Mrs Lirriper's Lodgings/ Mrs Lirriper'

by Charles Dicken

MRS. LIRRIPER'S LODGINGS

CHAPTER I

HOW MRS. LIRRIPER CARRIED ON THE BUSINESS

Whoever would begin to be worried with letting Lodgings that wasn't a lone woman with a living to get is a thing inconceivable to me, my dear; excuse the familiarity, but it comes natural to me in my own little room, when wishing to open my mind to those that I can trust, and I should be truly thankful if they were all mankind, but such is not so, for have but a Furnished bill in the window and your watch on the mantelpiece, and farewell to it if you turn your back for but a second, however gentlemanly the manners; nor is being of your own sex any safeguard, as I have reason, in the form of sugar-tongs to know, for that lady (and a fine woman she was) got me to run for a glass of water, on the plea of going to be confined, which certainly turned out true, but it was in the Station-house.

Number Eighty-one Norfolk Street, Strand--situated midway between the City and St. James's, and within five minutes' walk of the principal places of public amusement--is my address. I have rented this house many years, as the parish rate-books will testify; and I could wish my landlord was as alive to the fact as I am myself; but no, bless you, not a half a pound of paint to save his life, nor so much, my dear, as a tile upon the roof, though on your bended knees.

My dear, you never have found Number Eighty-one Norfolk Street Strand advertised in Bradshaw's Railway Guide, and with the blessing of Heaven you never will or shall so find it. Some there are who do not think it lowering themselves to make their names that cheap, and even going the lengths of a portrait of the house not like it with a blot in every window and a coach and four at the door, but what will suit Wozenham's lower down on the other side of the way will not suit me, Miss Wozenham having her opinions and me having mine, though when it comes to systematic underbidding capable of being proved on oath in a court of justice and taking the form of "If Mrs. Lirriper names eighteen shillings a week, I name fifteen and six," it then comes to a settlement between yourself and your conscience, supposing for the sake of argument your name to be Wozenham, which I am well aware it is not or my opinion of you would be greatly lowered, and as to airy bedrooms and a night-porter in constant attendance the less said the better, the bedrooms being stuffy and the porter stuff.

It is forty years ago since me and my poor Lirriper got married at St. Clement's Danes, where I now have a sitting in a very pleasant pew with genteel company and my own hassock, and being partial to evening service not too crowded. My poor Lirriper was a handsome figure of a man, with a beaming eye and a voice as mellow as a musical instrument made of honey and steel, but he had ever been a free liver being in the commercial travelling line and travelling what he called a limekiln road--"a dry road, Emma my dear," my poor Lirriper says to me, "where I have to lay the dust with one drink or another all day long and half the night, and it wears me Emma"--and this led to his running through a good deal and might have run through the turnpike too when that dreadful horse that never would stand still for a single instant set off, but for its being night and the gate shut and consequently took his wheel, my poor Lirriper and the gig smashed to atoms and never spoke afterwards. He was a handsome figure of a man, and a man with a jovial heart and a sweet temper; but if they had come up then they never could have given you the mellowness of his voice, and indeed I consider photographs wanting in mellowness as a general rule and making you look like a new-ploughed field.

My poor Lirriper being behindhand with the world and being buried at Hatfield church in Hertfordshire, not that it was his native place but that he had a liking for the Salisbury Arms where we went upon our wedding-day and passed as happy a fortnight as ever happy was, I went round to the creditors and I says "Gentlemen I am acquainted with the fact that I am not answerable for my late husband's debts but I wish to pay them for I am his lawful wife and his good name is dear to me. I am going into the Lodgings gentlemen as a business and if I prosper every farthing that my late husband owed shall be paid for the sake of the love I bore him, by this right hand." It took a long time to do but it was done, and the silver cream-jug which is between ourselves and the bed and the mattress in my room up-stairs (or it would have found legs so sure as ever the Furnished bill was up) being presented by the gentlemen engraved "To Mrs. Lirriper a mark of grateful respect for her honourable conduct" gave me a turn which was too much for my feelings, till Mr. Betley which at that time had the parlours and loved his joke says "Cheer up Mrs. Lirriper, you should feel as if it was only your christening and they were your godfathers and godmothers which did promise for you." And it brought me round, and I don't mind confessing to you my dear that I then put a sandwich and a drop of sherry in a little basket and went down to Hatfield church-yard outside the coach and kissed my hand and laid it with a kind of proud and swelling love on my husband's grave, though bless you it had taken me so long to clear his name that my wedding-ring was worn quite fine and smooth when I laid it on the green green waving grass.

I am an old woman now and my good looks are gone but that's me my dear over the plate-warmer and considered like in the times when you used to pay two guineas on ivory and took your chance pretty much how you came out, which made you very careful how you left it about afterwards because people were turned so red and uncomfortable by mostly guessing it was somebody else quite different, and there was once a certain person that had put his money in a hop business that came in one morning to pay his rent and his respects being the second floor that would have taken it down from its hook and put it in his breast-pocket--you understand my dear--for the L, he says of the original--only there was no mellowness in HIS voice and I wouldn't let him, but his opinion of it you may gather from his saying to it "Speak to me Emma!" which was far from a rational observation no doubt but still a tribute to its being a likeness, and I think myself it WAS like me when I was young and wore that sort of stays.

But it was about the Lodgings that I was intending to hold forth and certainly I ought to know something of the business having been in it so long, for it was early in the second year of my married life that I lost my poor Lirriper and I set up at Islington directly afterwards and afterwards came here, being two houses and eight-and- thirty years and some losses and a deal of experience.

Girls are your first trial after fixtures and they try you even worse than what I call the Wandering Christians, though why THEY should roam the earth looking for bills and then coming in and viewing the apartments and stickling about terms and never at all wanting them or dreaming of taking them being already provided, is, a mystery I should be thankful to have explained if by any miracle it could be. It's wonderful they live so long and thrive so on it but I suppose the exercise makes it healthy, knocking so much and going from house to house and up and down-stairs all day, and then their pretending to be so particular and punctual is a most astonishing thing, looking at their watches and saying "Could you give me the refusal of the rooms till twenty minutes past eleven the day after to-morrow in the forenoon, and supposing it to be considered essential by my friend from the country could there be a small iron bedstead put in the little room upon the stairs?" Why when I was new to it my dear I used to consider before I promised and to make my mind anxious with calculations and to get quite wearied out with disappointments, but now I says "Certainly by all means" well knowing it's a Wandering Christian and I shall hear no more about it, indeed by this time I know most of the Wandering Christians by sight as well as they know me, it being the habit of each individual revolving round London in that capacity to come back about twice a year, and it's very remarkable that it runs in families and the children grow up to it, but even were it otherwise I should no sooner hear of the friend from the country which is a certain sign than I should nod and say to myself You're a Wandering Christian, though whether they are (as I HAVE heard) persons of small property with a taste for regular employment and frequent change of scene I cannot undertake to tell you.

Girls as I was beginning to remark are one of your first and your lasting troubles, being like your teeth which begin with convulsions and never cease tormenting you from the time you cut them till they cut you, and then you don't want to part with them which seems hard but we must all succumb or buy artificial, and even where you get a will nine times out of ten you'll get a dirty face with it and naturally lodgers do not like good society to be shown in with a smear of black across the nose or a smudgy eyebrow. Where they pick the black up is a mystery I cannot solve, as in the case of the willingest girl that ever came into a house half-starved poor thing, a girl so willing that I called her Willing Sophy down upon her knees scrubbing early and late and ever cheerful but always smiling with a black face. And I says to Sophy, "Now Sophy my good girl have a regular day for your stoves and keep the width of the Airy between yourself and the blacking and do not brush your hair with the bottoms of the saucepans and do not meddle with the snuffs of the candles and it stands to reason that it can no longer be" yet there it was and always on her nose, which turning up and being broad at the end seemed to boast of it and caused warning from a steady gentleman and excellent lodger with breakfast by the week but a little irritable and use of a sitting-room when required, his words being "Mrs. Lirriper I have arrived at the point of admitting that the Black is a man and a brother, but only in a natural form and when it can't be got off." Well consequently I put poor Sophy on to other work and forbid her answering the door or answering a bell on any account but she was so unfortunately willing that nothing would stop her flying up the kitchen-stairs whenever a bell was heard to tingle. I put it to her "O Sophy Sophy for goodness' goodness' sake where does it come from?" To which that poor unlucky willing mortal--bursting out crying to see me so vexed replied "I took a deal of black into me ma'am when I was a small child being much neglected and I think it must be, that it works out," so it continuing to work out of that poor thing and not having another fault to find with her I says "Sophy what do you seriously think of my helping you away to New South Wales where it might not be noticed?" Nor did I ever repent the money which was well spent, for she married the ship's cook on the voyage (himself a Mulotter) and did well and lived happy, and so far as ever I heard it was NOT noticed in a new state of society to her dying day.

In what way Miss Wozenham lower down on the other side of the way reconciled it to her feelings as a lady (which she is not) to entice Mary Anne Perkinsop from my service is best known to herself, I do not know and I do not wish to know how opinions are formed at Wozenham's on any point. But Mary Anne Perkinsop although I behaved handsomely to her and she behaved unhandsomely to me was worth her weight in gold as overawing lodgers without driving them away, for lodgers would be far more sparing of their bells with Mary Anne than I ever knew them to be with Maid or Mistress, which is a great triumph especially when accompanied with a cast in the eye and a bag of bones, but it was the steadiness of her way with them through her father's having failed in Pork. It was Mary Anne's looking so respectable in her person and being so strict in her spirits that conquered the tea-and-sugarest gentleman (for he weighed them both in a pair of scales every morning) that I have ever had to deal with and no lamb grew meeker, still it afterwards came round to me that Miss Wozenham happening to pass and seeing Mary Anne take in the milk of a milkman that made free in a rosy-faced way (I think no worse of him) with every girl in the street but was quite frozen up like the statue at Charing-cross by her, saw Mary Anne's value in the lodging business and went as high as one pound per quarter more, consequently Mary Anne with not a word betwixt us says "If you will provide yourself Mrs. Lirriper in a month from this day I have already done the same," which hurt me and I said so, and she then hurt me more by insinuating that her father having failed in Pork had laid her open to it.

My dear I do assure you it's a harassing thing to know what kind of girls to give the preference to, for if they are lively they get bell'd off their legs and if they are sluggish you suffer from it yourself in complaints and if they are sparkling-eyed they get made love to, and if they are smart in their persons they try on your Lodgers' bonnets and if they are musical I defy you to keep them away from bands and organs, and allowing for any difference you like in their heads their heads will be always out of window just the same. And then what the gentlemen like in girls the ladies don't, which is fruitful hot water for all parties, and then there's temper though such a temper as Caroline Maxey's I hope not often. A good- looking black-eyed girl was Caroline and a comely-made girl to your cost when she did break out and laid about her, as took place first and last through a new-married couple come to see London in the first floor and the lady very high and it WAS supposed not liking the good looks of Caroline having none of her own to spare, but anyhow she did try Caroline though that was no excuse. So one afternoon Caroline comes down into the kitchen flushed and flashing, and she says to me "Mrs. Lirriper that woman in the first has aggravated me past bearing," I says "Caroline keep your temper," Caroline says with a curdling laugh "Keep my temper? You're right Mrs. Lirriper, so I will. Capital D her!" bursts out Caroline (you might have struck me into the centre of the earth with a feather when she said it) "I'll give her a touch of the temper that I keep!" Caroline downs with her hair my dear, screeches and rushes up- stairs, I following as fast as my trembling legs could bear me, but before I got into the room the dinner-cloth and pink-and-white service all dragged off upon the floor with a crash and the new-married couple on their backs in the firegrate, him with the shovel and tongs and a dish of cucumber across him and a mercy it was summer-time. "Caroline" I says "be calm," but she catches off my cap and tears it in her teeth as she passes me, then pounces on the new-married lady makes her a bundle of ribbons takes her by the two ears and knocks the back of her head upon the carpet Murder screaming all the time Policemen running down the street and Wozenham's windows (judge of my feelings when I came to know it) thrown up and Miss Wozenham calling out from the balcony with crocodile's tears "It's Mrs. Lirriper been overcharging somebody to madness-- she'll be murdered--I always thought so--Pleeseman save her!" My dear four of them and Caroline behind the chiffoniere attacking with the poker and when disarmed prize-fighting with her double fists, and down and up and up and down and dreadful! But I couldn't bear to see the poor young creature roughly handled and her hair torn when they got the better of her, and I says "Gentlemen Policemen pray remember that her sex is the sex of your mothers and sisters and your sweethearts, and God bless them and you!" And there she was sitting down on the ground handcuffed, taking breath against the skirting-board and them cool with their coats in strips, and all she says was "Mrs. Lirriper I'm sorry as ever I touched you, for you're a kind motherly old thing," and it made me think that I had often wished I had been a mother indeed and how would my heart have felt if I had been the mother of that girl! Well you know it turned out at the Police-office that she had done it before, and she had her clothes away and was sent to prison, and when she was to come out I trotted off to the gate in the evening with just a morsel of jelly in that little basket of mine to give her a mite of strength to face the world again, and there I met with a very decent mother waiting for her son through bad company and a stubborn one he was with his half-boots not laced. So out came Caroline and I says "Caroline come along with me and sit down under the wall where it's retired and eat a little trifle that I have brought with me to do you good," and she throws her arms round my neck and says sobbing "O why were you never a mother when there are such mothers as there are!" she says, and in half a minute more she begins to laugh and says "Did I really tear your cap to shreds?" and when I told her "You certainly did so Caroline" she laughed again and said while she patted my face "Then why do you wear such queer old caps you dear old thing? if you hadn't worn such queer old caps I don't think I should have done it even then." Fancy the girl! Nothing could get out of her what she was going to do except O she would do well enough, and we parted she being very thankful and kissing my hands, and I nevermore saw or heard of that girl, except that I shall always believe that a very genteel cap which was brought anonymous to me one Saturday night in an oilskin basket by a most impertinent young sparrow of a monkey whistling with dirty shoes on the clean steps and playing the harp on the Airy railings with a hoop-stick came from Caroline.

What you lay yourself open to my dear in the way of being the object of uncharitable suspicions when you go into the Lodging business I have not the words to tell you, but never was I so dishonourable as to have two keys nor would I willingly think it even of Miss Wozenham lower down on the other side of the way sincerely hoping that it may not be, though doubtless at the same time money cannot come from nowhere and it is not reason to suppose that Bradshaws put it in for love be it blotty as it may. It IS a hardship hurting to the feelings that Lodgers open their minds so wide to the idea that you are trying to get the better of them and shut their minds so close to the idea that they are trying to get the better of you, but as Major Jackman says to me, "I know the ways of this circular world Mrs. Lirriper, and that's one of 'em all round it" and many is the little ruffle in my mind that the Major has smoothed, for he is a clever man who has seen much. Dear dear, thirteen years have passed though it seems but yesterday since I was sitting with my glasses on at the open front parlour window one evening in August (the parlours being then vacant) reading yesterday's paper my eyes for print being poor though still I am thankful to say a long sight at a distance, when I hear a gentleman come posting across the road and up the street in a dreadful rage talking to himself in a fury and d'ing and c'ing somebody. "By George!" says he out loud and clutching his walking-stick, "I'll go to Mrs. Lirriper's. Which is Mrs. Lirriper's?" Then looking round and seeing me he flourishes his hat right off his head as if I had been the queen and he says, "Excuse the intrusion Madam, but pray Madam can you tell me at what number in this street there resides a well-known and much-respected lady by the name of Lirriper?" A little flustered though I must say gratified I took off my glasses and courtesied and said "Sir, Mrs. Lirriper is your humble servant." "Astonishing!" says he. "A million pardons! Madam, may I ask you to have the kindness to direct one of your domestics to open the door to a gentleman in search of apartments, by the name of Jackman?" I had never heard the name but a politer gentleman I never hope to see, for says he, "Madam I am shocked at your opening the door yourself to no worthier a fellow than Jemmy Jackman. After you Madam. I never precede a lady." Then he comes into the parlours and he sniffs, and he says "Hah! These are parlours! Not musty cupboards" he says "but parlours, and no smell of coal-sacks." Now my dear it having been remarked by some inimical to the whole neighbourhood that it always smells of coal-sacks which might prove a drawback to Lodgers if encouraged, I says to the Major gently though firmly that I think he is referring to Arundel or Surrey or Howard but not Norfolk. "Madam" says he "I refer to Wozenham's lower down over the way-- Madam you can form no notion what Wozenham's is--Madam it is a vast coal-sack, and Miss Wozenham has the principles and manners of a female heaver--Madam from the manner in which I have heard her mention you I know she has no appreciation of a lady, and from the manner in which she has conducted herself towards me I know she has no appreciation of a gentleman--Madam my name is Jackman--should you require any other reference than what I have already said, I name the Bank of England--perhaps you know it!" Such was the beginning of the Major's occupying the parlours and from that hour to this the same and a most obliging Lodger and punctual in all respects except one irregular which I need not particularly specify, but made up for by his being a protection and at all times ready to fill in the papers of the Assessed Taxes and Juries and that, and once collared a young man with the drawing-room clock under his coat, and once on the parapets with his own hands and blankets put out the kitchen chimney and afterwards attending the summons made a most eloquent speech against the Parish before the magistrates and saved the engine, and ever quite the gentleman though passionate. And certainly Miss Wozenham's detaining the trunks and umbrella was not in a liberal spirit though it may have been according to her rights in law or an act I would myself have stooped to, the Major being so much the gentleman that though he is far from tall he seems almost so when he has his shirt-frill out and his frock-coat on and his hat with the curly brims, and in what service he was I cannot truly tell you my dear whether Militia or Foreign, for I never heard him even name himself as Major but always simple "Jemmy Jackman" and once soon after he came when I felt it my duty to let him know that Miss Wozenham had put it about that he was no Major and I took the liberty of adding "which you are sir" his words were "Madam at any rate I am not a Minor, and sufficient for the day is the evil thereof" which cannot be denied to be the sacred truth, nor yet his military ways of having his boots with only the dirt brushed off taken to him in the front parlour every morning on a clean plate and varnishing them himself with a little sponge and a saucer and a whistle in a whisper so sure as ever his breakfast is ended, and so neat his ways that it never soils his linen which is scrupulous though more in quality than quantity, neither that nor his mustachios which to the best of my belief are done at the same time and which are as black and shining as his boots, his head of hair being a lovely white.

It was the third year nearly up of the Major's being in the parlours that early one morning in the month of February when Parliament was coming on and you may therefore suppose a number of impostors were about ready to take hold of anything they could get, a gentleman and a lady from the country came in to view the Second, and I well remember that I had been looking out of window and had watched them and the heavy sleet driving down the street together looking for bills. I did not quite take to the face of the gentleman though he was good-looking too but the lady was a very pretty young thing and delicate, and it seemed too rough for her to be out at all though she had only come from the Adelphi Hotel which would not have been much above a quarter of a mile if the weather had been less severe. Now it did so happen my dear that I had been forced to put five shillings weekly additional on the second in consequence of a loss from running away full dressed as if going out to a dinner-party, which was very artful and had made me rather suspicious taking it along with Parliament, so when the gentleman proposed three months certain and the money in advance and leave then reserved to renew on the same terms for six months more, I says I was not quite certain but that I might have engaged myself to another party but would step down-stairs and look into it if they would take a seat. They took a seat and I went down to the handle of the Major's door that I had already began to consult finding it a great blessing, and I knew by his whistling in a whisper that he was varnishing his boots which was generally considered private, however he kindly calls out "If it's you, Madam, come in," and I went in and told him.

"Well, Madam," says the Major rubbing his nose--as I did fear at the moment with the black sponge but it was only his knuckle, he being always neat and dexterous with his fingers--"well, Madam, I suppose you would be glad of the money?"

I was delicate of saying "Yes" too out, for a little extra colour rose into the Major's cheeks and there was irregularity which I will not particularly specify in a quarter which I will not name.

"I am of opinion, Madam," says the Major, "that when money is ready for you--when it is ready for you, Mrs. Lirriper--you ought to take it. What is there against it, Madam, in this case up-stairs?"

"I really cannot say there is anything against it, sir, still I thought I would consult you."

"You said a newly-married couple, I think, Madam?" says the Major.

I says "Ye-es. Evidently. And indeed the young lady mentioned to me in a casual way that she had not been married many months."

The Major rubbed his nose again and stirred the varnish round and round in its little saucer with his piece of sponge and took to his whistling in a whisper for a few moments. Then he says "You would call it a Good Let, Madam?"

"O certainly a Good Let sir."

"Say they renew for the additional six months. Would it put you about very much Madam if--if the worst was to come to the worst?" said the Major.

"Well I hardly know," I says to the Major. "It depends upon circumstances. Would YOU object Sir for instance?"

"I?" says the Major. "Object? Jemmy Jackman? Mrs. Lirriper close with the proposal."

So I went up-stairs and accepted, and they came in next day which was Saturday and the Major was so good as to draw up a Memorandum of an agreement in a beautiful round hand and expressions that sounded to me equally legal and military, and Mr. Edson signed it on the Monday morning and the Major called upon Mr. Edson on the Tuesday and Mr. Edson called upon the Major on the Wednesday and the Second and the parlours were as friendly as could be wished.

The three months paid for had run out and we had got without any fresh overtures as to payment into May my dear, when there came an obligation upon Mr. Edson to go a business expedition right across the Isle of Man, which fell quite unexpected upon that pretty little thing and is not a place that according to my views is particularly in the way to anywhere at any time but that may be a matter of opinion. So short a notice was it that he was to go next day, and dreadfully she cried poor pretty, and I am sure I cried too when I saw her on the cold pavement in the sharp east wind--it being a very backward spring that year--taking a last leave of him with her pretty bright hair blowing this way and that and her arms clinging round his neck and him saying "There there there. Now let me go Peggy." And by that time it was plain that what the Major had been so accommodating as to say he would not object to happening in the house, would happen in it, and I told her as much when he was gone while I comforted her with my arm up the staircase, for I says "You will soon have others to keep up for my pretty and you must think of that."

His letter never came when it ought to have come and what she went through morning after morning when the postman brought none for her the very postman himself compassionated when she ran down to the door, and yet we cannot wonder at its being calculated to blunt the feelings to have all the trouble of other people's letters and none of the pleasure and doing it oftener in the mud and mizzle than not and at a rate of wages more resembling Little Britain than Great. But at last one morning when she was too poorly to come running down-stairs he says to me with a pleased look in his face that made me next to love the man in his uniform coat though he was dripping wet "I have taken you first in the street this morning Mrs. Lirriper, for here's the one for Mrs. Edson." I went up to her bedroom with it as fast as ever I could go, and she sat up in bed when she saw it and kissed it and tore it open and then a blank stare came upon her. "It's very short!" she says lifting her large eyes to my face. "O Mrs. Lirriper it's very short!" I says "My dear Mrs. Edson no doubt that's because your husband hadn't time to write more just at that time." "No doubt, no doubt," says she, and puts her two hands on her face and turns round in her bed.

I shut her softly in and I crept down-stairs and I tapped at the Major's door, and when the Major having his thin slices of bacon in his own Dutch oven saw me he came out of his chair and put me down on the sofa. "Hush!" says he, "I see something's the matter. Don't speak--take time." I says "O Major I'm afraid there's cruel work up-stairs." "Yes yes" says he "I had begun to be afraid of it--take time." And then in opposition to his own words he rages out frightfully, and says "I shall never forgive myself Madam, that I, Jemmy Jackman, didn't see it all that morning--didn't go straight up-stairs when my boot-sponge was in my hand--didn't force it down his throat--and choke him dead with it on the spot!"

The Major and me agreed when we came to ourselves that just at present we could do no more than take on to suspect nothing and use our best endeavours to keep that poor young creature quiet, and what I ever should have done without the Major when it got about among the organ-men that quiet was our object is unknown, for he made lion and tiger war upon them to that degree that without seeing it I could not have believed it was in any gentleman to have such a power of bursting out with fire-irons walking-sticks water-jugs coals potatoes off his table the very hat off his head, and at the same time so furious in foreign languages that they would stand with their handles half-turned fixed like the Sleeping Ugly--for I cannot say Beauty.

Ever to see the postman come near the house now gave me such I fear that it was a reprieve when he went by, but in about another ten days or a fortnight he says again, "Here's one for Mrs. Edson.--Is she pretty well?" "She is pretty well postman, but not well enough to rise so early as she used" which was so far gospel-truth.

I carried the letter in to the Major at his breakfast and I says tottering "Major I have not the courage to take it up to her."

"It's an ill-looking villain of a letter," says the Major.

"I have not the courage Major" I says again in a tremble "to take it up to her."

After seeming lost in consideration for some moments the Major says, raising his head as if something new and useful had occurred to his mind "Mrs. Lirriper, I shall never forgive myself that I, Jemmy Jackman, didn't go straight up-stairs that morning when my boot- sponge was in my hand--and force it down his throat--and choke him dead with it."

"Major" I says a little hasty "you didn't do it which is a blessing, for it would have done no good and I think your sponge was better employed on your own honourable boots."

So we got to be rational, and planned that I should tap at her bedroom door and lay the letter on the mat outside and wait on the upper landing for what might happen, and never was gunpowder cannon- balls or shells or rockets more dreaded than that dreadful letter was by me as I took it to the second floor.

A terrible loud scream sounded through the house the minute after she had opened it, and I found her on the floor lying as if her life was gone. My dear I never looked at the face of the letter which was lying, open by her, for there was no occasion.

Everything I needed to bring her round the Major brought up with his own hands, besides running out to the chemist's for what was not in the house and likewise having the fiercest of all his many skirmishes with a musical instrument representing a ball-room I do not know in what particular country and company waltzing in and out at folding-doors with rolling eyes. When after a long time I saw her coming to, I slipped on the landing till I heard her cry, and then I went in and says cheerily "Mrs. Edson you're not well my dear and it's not to be wondered at," as if I had not been in before. Whether she believed or disbelieved I cannot say and it would signify nothing if I could, but I stayed by her for hours and then she God ever blesses me! and says she will try to rest for her head is bad.

"Major," I whispers, looking in at the parlours, "I beg and pray of you don't go out."

The Major whispers, "Madam, trust me I will do no such a thing. How is she?"

I says "Major the good Lord above us only knows what burns and rages in her poor mind. I left her sitting at her window. I am going to sit at mine."

It came on afternoon and it came on evening. Norfolk is a delightful street to lodge in--provided you don't go lower down--but of a summer evening when the dust and waste paper lie in it and stray children play in it and a kind of a gritty calm and bake settles on it and a peal of church-bells is practising in the neighbourhood it is a trifle dull, and never have I seen it since at such a time and never shall I see it evermore at such a time without seeing the dull June evening when that forlorn young creature sat at her open corner window on the second and me at my open corner window (the other corner) on the third. Something merciful, something wiser and better far than my own self, had moved me while it was yet light to sit in my bonnet and shawl, and as the shadows fell and the tide rose I could sometimes--when I put out my head and looked at her window below--see that she leaned out a little looking down the street. It was just settling dark when I saw HER in the street.

So fearful of losing sight of her that it almost stops my breath while I tell it, I went down-stairs faster than I ever moved in all my life and only tapped with my hand at the Major's door in passing it and slipping out. She was gone already. I made the same speed down the street and when I came to the corner of Howard Street I saw that she had turned it and was there plain before me going towards the west. O with what a thankful heart I saw her going along!

She was quite unacquainted with London and had very seldom been out for more than an airing in our own street where she knew two or three little children belonging to neighbours and had sometimes stood among them at the street looking at the water. She must be going at hazard I knew, still she kept the by-streets quite correctly as long as they would serve her, and then turned up into the Strand. But at every corner I could see her head turned one way, and that way was always the river way.

It may have been only the darkness and quiet of the Adelphi that caused her to strike into it but she struck into it much as readily as if she had set out to go there, which perhaps was the case. She went straight down to the Terrace and along it and looked over the iron rail, and I often woke afterwards in my own bed with the horror of seeing her do it. The desertion of the wharf below and the flowing of the high water there seemed to settle her purpose. She looked about as if to make out the way down, and she struck out the right way or the wrong way--I don't know which, for I don't know the place before or since--and I followed her the way she went.

It was noticeable that all this time she never once looked back. But there was now a great change in the manner of her going, and instead of going at a steady quick walk with her arms folded before her,--among the dark dismal arches she went in a wild way with her arms opened wide, as if they were wings and she was flying to her death.

We were on the wharf and she stopped. I stopped. I saw her hands at her bonnet-strings, and I rushed between her and the brink and took her round the waist with both my arms. She might have drowned me, I felt then, but she could never have got quit of me.

Down to that moment my mind had been all in a maze and not half an idea had I had in it what I should say to her, but the instant I touched her it came to me like magic and I had my natural voice and my senses and even almost my breath.

"Mrs. Edson!" I says "My dear! Take care. How ever did you lose your way and stumble on a dangerous place like this? Why you must have come here by the most perplexing streets in all London. No wonder you are lost, I'm sure. And this place too! Why I thought nobody ever got here, except me to order my coals and the Major in the parlours to smoke his cigar!"--for I saw that blessed man close by, pretending to it.

"Hah--Hah--Hum!" coughs the Major.

"And good gracious me" I says," why here he is!"

"Halloa! who goes there?" says the Major in a military manner.

"Well!" I says, "if this don't beat everything! Don't you know us Major Jackman?"

"Halloa!" says the Major. "Who calls on Jemmy Jackman?" (and more out of breath he was, and did it less like life than I should have expected.)

"Why here's Mrs. Edson Major" I says, "strolling out to cool her poor head which has been very bad, has missed her way and got lost, and Goodness knows where she might have got to but for me coming here to drop an order into my coal merchant's letter-box and you coming here to smoke your cigar!--And you really are not well enough my dear" I says to her "to be half so far from home without me. And your arm will be very acceptable I am sure Major" I says to him "and I know she may lean upon it as heavy as she likes." And now we had both got her--thanks be Above!--one on each side.

She was all in a cold shiver and she so continued till I laid her on her own bed, and up to the early morning she held me by the hand and moaned and moaned "O wicked, wicked, wicked!" But when at last I made believe to droop my head and be overpowered with a dead sleep, I heard that poor young creature give such touching and such humble thanks for being preserved from taking her own life in her madness that I thought I should have cried my eyes out on the counterpane and I knew she was safe.

Being well enough to do and able to afford it, me and the Major laid our little plans next day while she was asleep worn out, and so I says to her as soon as I could do it nicely:

"Mrs. Edson my dear, when Mr. Edson paid me the rent for these farther six months--"

She gave a start and I felt her large eyes look at me, but I went on with it and with my needlework.

"--I can't say that I am quite sure I dated the receipt right. Could you let me look at it?"

She laid her frozen cold hand upon mine and she looked through me when I was forced to look up from my needlework, but I had taken the precaution of having on my spectacles.

"I have no receipt" says she.

"Ah! Then he has got it" I says in a careless way. "It's of no great consequence. A receipt's a receipt."

From that time she always had hold of my hand when I could spare it which was generally only when I read to her, for of course she and me had our bits of needlework to plod at and neither of us was very handy at those little things, though I am still rather proud of my share in them too considering. And though she took to all I read to her, I used to fancy that next to what was taught upon the Mount she took most of all to His gentle compassion for us poor women and to His young life and to how His mother was proud of Him and treasured His sayings in her heart. She had a grateful look in her eyes that never never never will be out of mine until they are closed in my last sleep, and when I chanced to look at her without thinking of it I would always meet that look, and she would often offer me her trembling lip to kiss, much more like a little affectionate half broken-hearted child than ever I can imagine any grown person.

One time the trembling of this poor lip was so strong and her tears ran down so fast that I thought she was going to tell me all her woe, so I takes her two hands in mine and I says:

"No my dear not now, you had best not try to do it now. Wait for better times when you have got over this and are strong, and then you shall tell me whatever you will. Shall it be agreed?"

With our hands still joined she nodded her head many times, and she lifted my hands and put them to her lips and to her bosom. "Only one word now my dear" I says. "Is there any one?"

She looked inquiringly "Any one?"

"That I can go to?"

She shook her head.

"No one that I can bring?"

She shook her head.

"No one is wanted by ME my dear. Now that may be considered past and gone."

Not much more than a week afterwards--for this was far on in the time of our being so together--I was bending over at her bedside with my ear down to her lips, by turns listening for her breath and looking for a sign of life in her face. At last it came in a solemn way--not in a flash but like a kind of pale faint light brought very slow to the face.

She said something to me that had no sound in it, but I saw she asked me:

"Is this death?"

And I says:

"Poor dear poor dear, I think it is."

Knowing somehow that she wanted me to move her weak right hand, I took it and laid it on her breast and then folded her other hand upon it, and she prayed a good good prayer and I joined in it poor me though there were no words spoke. Then I brought the baby in its wrappers from where it lay, and I says:

"My dear this is sent to a childless old woman. This is for me to take care of."

The trembling lip was put up towards my face for the last time, and I dearly kissed it.

"Yes my dear," I says. "Please God! Me and the Major."

I don't know how to tell it right, but I saw her soul brighten and leap up, and get free and fly away in the grateful look.

* * *

So this is the why and wherefore of its coming to pass my dear that we called him Jemmy, being after the Major his own godfather with Lirriper for a surname being after myself, and never was a dear child such a brightening thing in a Lodgings or such a playmate to his grandmother as Jemmy to this house and me, and always good and minding what he was told (upon the whole) and soothing for the temper and making everything pleasanter except when he grew old enough to drop his cap down Wozenham's Airy and they wouldn't hand it up to him, and being worked into a state I put on my best bonnet and gloves and parasol with the child in my hand and I says "Miss Wozenham I little thought ever to have entered your house but unless my grandson's cap is instantly restored, the laws of this country regulating the property of the Subject shall at length decide betwixt yourself and me, cost what it may." With a sneer upon her face which did strike me I must say as being expressive of two keys but it may have been a mistake and if there is any doubt let Miss Wozenham have the full benefit of it as is but right, she rang the bell and she says "Jane, is there a street-child's old cap down our Airy?" I says "Miss Wozenham before your housemaid answers that question you must allow me to inform you to your face that my grandson is NOT a street-child and is NOT in the habit of wearing old caps. In fact" I says "Miss Wozenham I am far from sure that my grandson's cap may not be newer than your own" which was perfectly savage in me, her lace being the commonest machine-make washed and torn besides, but I had been put into a state to begin with fomented by impertinence. Miss Wozenham says red in the face "Jane you heard my question, is there any child's cap down our Airy?" "Yes Ma'am" says Jane, "I think I did see some such rubbish a-lying there." "Then" says Miss Wozenham "let these visitors out, and then throw up that worthless article out of my premises." But here the child who had been staring at Miss Wozenham with all his eyes and more, frowns down his little eyebrows purses up his little mouth puts his chubby legs far apart turns his little dimpled fists round and round slowly over one another like a little coffee-mill, and says to her "Oo impdent to mi Gran, me tut oor hi!" "O!" says Miss Wozenham looking down scornfully at the Mite "this is not a street-child is it not! Really!" I bursts out laughing and I says "Miss Wozenham if this ain't a pretty sight to you I don't envy your feelings and I wish you good-day. Jemmy come along with Gran." And I was still in the best of humours though his cap came flying up into the street as if it had been just turned on out of the water-plug, and I went home laughing all the way, all owing to that dear boy.

The miles and miles that me and the Major have travelled with Jemmy in the dusk between the lights are not to be calculated, Jemmy driving on the coach-box which is the Major's brass-bound writing desk on the table, me inside in the easy-chair and the Major Guard up behind with a brown-paper horn doing it really wonderful. I do assure you my dear that sometimes when I have taken a few winks in my place inside the coach and have come half awake by the flashing light of the fire and have heard that precious pet driving and the Major blowing up behind to have the change of horses ready when we got to the Inn, I have half believed we were on the old North Road that my poor Lirriper knew so well. Then to see that child and the Major both wrapped up getting down to warm their feet and going stamping about and having glasses of ale out of the paper matchboxes on the chimney-piece is to see the Major enjoying it fully as much as the child I am very sure, and it's equal to any play when Coachee opens the coach-door to look in at me inside and say "Wery 'past that 'tage.--'Prightened old lady?"

But what my inexpressible feelings were when we lost that child can only be compared to the Major's which were not a shade better, through his straying out at five years old and eleven o'clock in the forenoon and never heard of by word or sign or deed till half-past nine at night, when the Major had gone to the Editor of the Times newspaper to put in an advertisement, which came out next day four- and-twenty hours after he was found, and which I mean always carefully to keep in my lavender drawer as the first printed account of him. The more the day got on, the more I got distracted and the Major too and both of us made worse by the composed ways of the police though very civil and obliging and what I must call their obstinacy in not entertaining the idea that he was stolen. "We mostly find Mum" says the sergeant who came round to comfort me, which he didn't at all and he had been one of the private constables in Caroline's time to which he referred in his opening words when he said "Don't give way to uneasiness in your mind Mum, it'll all come as right as my nose did when I got the same barked by that young woman in your second floor"--says this sergeant "we mostly find Mum as people ain't over-anxious to have what I may call second-hand children. YOU'LL get him back Mum." "O but my dear good sir" I says clasping my hands and wringing them and clasping them again "he is such an uncommon child!" "Yes Mum" says the sergeant, "we mostly find that too Mum. The question is what his clothes were worth." "His clothes" I says "were not worth much sir for he had only got his playing-dress on, but the dear child!--" "All right Mum" says the sergeant. "You'll get him back Mum. And even if he'd had his best clothes on, it wouldn't come to worse than his being found wrapped up in a cabbage-leaf, a shivering in a lane." His words pierced my heart like daggers and daggers, and me and the Major ran in and out like wild things all day long till the Major returning from his interview with the Editor of the Times at night rushes into my little room hysterical and squeezes my hand and wipes his eyes and says "Joy joy--officer in plain clothes came up on the steps as I was letting myself in--compose your feelings--Jemmy's found." Consequently I fainted away and when I came to, embraced the legs of the officer in plain clothes who seemed to be taking a kind of a quiet inventory in his mind of the property in my little room with brown whiskers, and I says "Blessings on you sir where is the Darling!" and he says "In Kennington Station House." I was dropping at his feet Stone at the image of that Innocence in cells with murderers when he adds "He followed the Monkey." I says deeming it slang language "O sir explain for a loving grandmother what Monkey!" He says "Him in the spangled cap with the strap under the chin, as won't keep on--him as sweeps the crossings on a round table and don't want to draw his sabre more than he can help." Then I understood it all and most thankfully thanked him, and me and the Major and him drove over to Kennington and there we found our boy lying quite comfortable before a blazing fire having sweetly played himself to sleep upon a small accordion nothing like so big as a flat-iron which they had been so kind as to lend him for the purpose and which it appeared had been stopped upon a very young person.

My dear the system upon which the Major commenced and as I may say perfected Jemmy's learning when he was so small that if the dear was on the other side of the table you had to look under it instead of over it to see him with his mother's own bright hair in beautiful curls, is a thing that ought to be known to the Throne and Lords and Commons and then might obtain some promotion for the Major which he well deserves and would be none the worse for (speaking between friends) L. S. D.-ically. When the Major first undertook his learning he says to me:

"I'm going Madam," he says "to make our child a Calculating Boy.

"Major," I says, "you terrify me and may do the pet a permanent injury you would never forgive yourself."

"Madam," says the Major, "next to my regret that when I had my boot-sponge in my hand, I didn't choke that scoundrel with it--on the spot--"

"There! For Gracious' sake," I interrupts, "let his conscience find him without sponges."

"--I say next to that regret, Madam," says the Major "would be the regret with which my breast," which he tapped, "would be surcharged if this fine mind was not early cultivated. But mark me Madam," says the Major holding up his forefinger "cultivated on a principle that will make it a delight."

"Major" I says "I will be candid with you and tell you openly that if ever I find the dear child fall off in his appetite I shall know it is his calculations and shall put a stop to them at two minutes' notice. Or if I find them mounting to his head" I says, "or striking anyways cold to his stomach or leading to anything approaching flabbiness in his legs, the result will be the same, but Major you are a clever man and have seen much and you love the child and are his own godfather, and if you feel a confidence in trying try."

"Spoken Madam" says the Major "like Emma Lirriper. All I have to ask, Madam, is that you will leave my godson and myself to make a week or two's preparations for surprising you, and that you will give me leave to have up and down any small articles not actually in use that I may require from the kitchen."

"From the kitchen Major?" I says half feeling as if he had a mind to cook the child.

"From the kitchen" says the Major, and smiles and swells, and at the same time looks taller.

So I passed my word and the Major and the dear boy were shut up together for half an hour at a time through a certain while, and never could I hear anything going on betwixt them but talking and laughing and Jemmy clapping his hands and screaming out numbers, so I says to myself "it has not harmed him yet" nor could I on examining the dear find any signs of it anywhere about him which was likewise a great relief. At last one day Jemmy brings me a card in joke in the Major's neat writing "The Messrs. Jemmy Jackman" for we had given him the Major's other name too "request the honour of Mrs. Lirriper's company at the Jackman Institution in the front parlour this evening at five, military time, to witness a few slight feats of elementary arithmetic." And if you'll believe me there in the front parlour at five punctual to the moment was the Major behind the Pembroke table with both leaves up and a lot of things from the kitchen tidily set out on old newspapers spread atop of it, and there was the Mite stood upon a chair with his rosy cheeks flushing and his eyes sparkling clusters of diamonds.

"Now Gran" says he, "oo tit down and don't oo touch ler people"--for he saw with every one of those diamonds of his that I was going to give him a squeeze.

"Very well sir" I says "I am obedient in this good company I am sure." And I sits down in the easy-chair that was put for me, shaking my sides.

But picture my admiration when the Major going on almost as quick as if he was conjuring sets out all the articles he names, and says "Three saucepans, an Italian iron, a hand-bell, a toasting-fork, a nutmeg-grater, four potlids, a spice-box, two egg-cups, and a chopping-board--how many?" and when that Mite instantly cries "Tifteen, tut down tive and carry ler 'toppin-board" and then claps his hands draws up his legs and dances on his chair.

My dear with the same astonishing ease and correctness him and the Major added up the tables chairs and sofy, the picters fenders and fire-irons their own selves me and the cat and the eyes in Miss Wozenham's head, and whenever the sum was done Young Roses and Diamonds claps his hands and draws up his legs and dances on his chair.

The pride of the Major! ("HERE'S a mind Ma'am!" he says to me behind his hand.)

Then he says aloud, "We now come to the next elementary rule,--which is called--"

"Umtraction!" cries Jemmy.

"Right," says the Major. "We have here a toasting-fork, a potato in its natural state, two potlids, one egg-cup, a wooden spoon, and two skewers, from which it is necessary for commercial purposes to subtract a sprat-gridiron, a small pickle-jar, two lemons, one pepper-castor, a blackbeetle-trap, and a knob of the dresser-drawer- -what remains?"

"Toatin-fork!" cries Jemmy.

"In numbers how many?" says the Major.

"One!" cries Jemmy.

("HERE'S a boy, Ma'am!" says the Major to me behind his hand.) Then the Major goes on:

"We now approach the next elementary rule,--which is entitled--"

"Tickleication" cries Jemmy.

"Correct" says the Major.

But my dear to relate to you in detail the way in which they multiplied fourteen sticks of firewood by two bits of ginger and a larding needle, or divided pretty well everything else there was on the table by the heater of the Italian iron and a chamber candlestick, and got a lemon over, would make my head spin round and round and round as it did at the time. So I says "if you'll excuse my addressing the chair Professor Jackman I think the period of the lecture has now arrived when it becomes necessary that I should take a good hug of this young scholar." Upon which Jemmy calls out from his station on the chair, "Gran oo open oor arms and me'll make a 'pring into 'em." So I opened my arms to him as I had opened my sorrowful heart when his poor young mother lay a dying, and he had his jump and we had a good long hug together and the Major prouder than any peacock says to me behind his hand, "You need not let him know it Madam" (which I certainly need not for the Major was quite audible) "but he IS a boy!"

In this way Jemmy grew and grew and went to day-school and continued under the Major too, and in summer we were as happy as the days were long, and in winter we were as happy as the days were short and there seemed to rest a Blessing on the Lodgings for they as good as Let themselves and would have done it if there had been twice the accommodation, when sore and hard against my will I one day says to the Major.

"Major you know what I am going to break to you. Our boy must go to boarding-school."

It was a sad sight to see the Major's countenance drop, and I pitied the good soul with all my heart.

"Yes Major" I says, "though he is as popular with the Lodgers as you are yourself and though he is to you and me what only you and me know, still it is in the course of things and Life is made of partings and we must part with our Pet."

Bold as I spoke, I saw two Majors and half-a-dozen fireplaces, and when the poor Major put one of his neat bright-varnished boots upon the fender and his elbow on his knee and his head upon his hand and rocked himself a little to and fro, I was dreadfully cut up.

"But" says I clearing my throat "you have so well prepared him Major--he has had such a Tutor in you--that he will have none of the first drudgery to go through. And he is so clever besides that he'll soon make his way to the front rank."

"He is a boy" says the Major--having sniffed--"that has not his like on the face of the earth."

"True as you say Major, and it is not for us merely for our own sakes to do anything to keep him back from being a credit and an ornament wherever he goes and perhaps even rising to be a great man, is it Major? He will have all my little savings when my work is done (being all the world to me) and we must try to make him a wise man and a good man, mustn't we Major?"

"Madam" says the Major rising "Jemmy Jackman is becoming an older file than I was aware of, and you put him to shame. You are thoroughly right Madam. You are simply and undeniably right.--And if you'll excuse me, I'll take a walk."

So the Major being gone out and Jemmy being at home, I got the child into my little room here and I stood him by my chair and I took his mother's own curls in my hand and I spoke to him loving and serious. And when I had reminded the darling how that he was now in his tenth year and when I had said to him about his getting on in life pretty much what I had said to the Major I broke to him how that we must have this same parting, and there I was forced to stop for there I saw of a sudden the well-remembered lip with its tremble, and it so brought back that time! But with the spirit that was in him he controlled it soon and he says gravely nodding through his tears, "I understand Gran--I know it MUST be, Gran--go on Gran, don't be afraid of ME." And when I had said all that ever I could think of, he turned his bright steady face to mine and he says just a little broken here and there "You shall see Gran that I can be a man and that I can do anything that is grateful and loving to you--and if I don't grow up to be what you would like to have me--I hope it will be--because I shall die." And with that he sat down by me and I went on to tell him of the school of which I had excellent recommendations and where it was and how many scholars and what games they played as I had heard and what length of holidays, to all of which he listened bright and clear. And so it came that at last he says "And now dear Gran let me kneel down here where I have been used to say my prayers and let me fold my face for just a minute in your gown and let me cry, for you have been more than father--more than mother--more than brothers sisters friends--to me!" And so he did cry and I too and we were both much the better for it.

From that time forth he was true to his word and ever blithe and ready, and even when me and the Major took him down into Lincolnshire he was far the gayest of the party though for sure and certain he might easily have been that, but he really was and put life into us only when it came to the last Good-bye, he says with a wistful look, "You wouldn't have me not really sorry would you Gran?" and when I says "No dear, Lord forbid!" he says "I am glad of that!" and ran in out of sight.

But now that the child was gone out of the Lodgings the Major fell into a regularly moping state. It was taken notice of by all the Lodgers that the Major moped. He hadn't even the same air of being rather tall than he used to have, and if he varnished his boots with a single gleam of interest it was as much as he did.

One evening the Major came into my little room to take a cup of tea and a morsel of buttered toast and to read Jemmy's newest letter which had arrived that afternoon (by the very same postman more than middle-aged upon the Beat now), and the letter raising him up a little I says to the Major:

"Major you mustn't get into a moping way."

The Major shook his head. "Jemmy Jackman Madam," he says with a deep sigh, "is an older file than I thought him."

"Moping is not the way to grow younger Major."

"My dear Madam," says the Major, "is there ANY way of growing younger?"

Feeling that the Major was getting rather the best of that point I made a diversion to another.

"Thirteen years! Thir-teen years! Many Lodgers have come and gone, in the thirteen years that you have lived in the parlours Major."

"Hah!" says the Major warming. "Many Madam, many."

"And I should say you have been familiar with them all?"

"As a rule (with its exceptions like all rules) my dear Madam" says the Major, "they have honoured me with their acquaintance, and not unfrequently with their confidence."

Watching the Major as he drooped his white head and stroked his black mustachios and moped again, a thought which I think must have been going about looking for an owner somewhere dropped into my old noddle if you will excuse the expression.

"The walls of my Lodgings" I says in a casual way--for my dear it is of no use going straight at a man who mopes--"might have something to tell if they could tell it."

The Major neither moved nor said anything but I saw he was attending with his shoulders my dear--attending with his shoulders to what I said. In fact I saw that his shoulders were struck by it.

"The dear boy was always fond of story-books" I went on, like as if I was talking to myself. "I am sure this house--his own home--might write a story or two for his reading one day or another."

The Major's shoulders gave a dip and a curve and his head came up in his shirt-collar. The Major's head came up in his shirt-collar as I hadn't seen it come up since Jemmy went to school.

"It is unquestionable that in intervals of cribbage and a friendly rubber, my dear Madam," says the Major, "and also over what used to be called in my young times--in the salad days of Jemmy Jackman--the social glass, I have exchanged many a reminiscence with your Lodgers."

My remark was--I confess I made it with the deepest and artfullest of intentions--"I wish our dear boy had heard them!"

"Are you serious Madam?" asked the Major starting and turning full round.

"Why not Major?"

"Madam" says the Major, turning up one of his cuffs, "they shall be written for him."

"Ah! Now you speak" I says giving my hands a pleased clap. "Now you are in a way out of moping Major!"

"Between this and my holidays--I mean the dear boy's" says the Major turning up his other cuff, "a good deal may be done towards it."

"Major you are a clever man and you have seen much and not a doubt of it."

"I'll begin," says the Major looking as tall as ever he did, "to- morrow."

My dear the Major was another man in three days and he was himself again in a week and he wrote and wrote and wrote with his pen scratching like rats behind the wainscot, and whether he had many grounds to go upon or whether he did at all romance I cannot tell you, but what he has written is in the left-hand glass closet of the little bookcase close behind you.

CHAPTER II

--HOW THE PARLOURS ADDED A FEW WORDS

I have the honour of presenting myself by the name of Jackman. I esteem it a proud privilege to go down to posterity through the instrumentality of the most remarkable boy that ever lived,--by the name of JEMMY JACKMAN LIRRIPER,--and of my most worthy and most highly respected friend, Mrs. Emma Lirriper, of Eighty-one, Norfolk Street, Strand, in the County of Middlesex, in the United Kingdom of Great Britain and Ireland.

It is not for me to express the rapture with which we received that dear and eminently remarkable boy, on the occurrence of his first Christmas holidays. Suffice it to observe that when he came flying into the house with two splendid prizes (Arithmetic, and Exemplary Conduct), Mrs. Lirriper and myself embraced with emotion, and instantly took him to the Play, where we were all three admirably entertained.

Nor is it to render homage to the virtues of the best of her good and honoured sex--whom, in deference to her unassuming worth, I will only here designate by the initials E. L.--that I add this record to the bundle of papers with which our, in a most distinguished degree, remarkable boy has expressed himself delighted, before re-consigning the same to the left-hand glass closet of Mrs. Lirriper's little bookcase.

Neither is it to obtrude the name of the old original superannuated obscure Jemmy Jackman, once (to his degradation) of Wozenham's, long (to his elevation) of Lirriper's. If I could be consciously guilty of that piece of bad taste, it would indeed be a work of supererogation, now that the name is borne by JEMMY JACKMAN LIRRIPER.

No, I take up my humble pen to register a little record of our strikingly remarkable boy, which my poor capacity regards as presenting a pleasant little picture of the dear boy's mind. The picture may be interesting to himself when he is a man.

Our first reunited Christmas-day was the most delightful one we have ever passed together. Jemmy was never silent for five minutes, except in church-time. He talked as we sat by the fire, he talked when we were out walking, he talked as we sat by the fire again, he talked incessantly at dinner, though he made a dinner almost as remarkable as himself. It was the spring of happiness in his fresh young heart flowing and flowing, and it fertilised (if I may be allowed so bold a figure) my much-esteemed friend, and J. J. the present writer.

There were only we three. We dined in my esteemed friend's little room, and our entertainment was perfect. But everything in the establishment is, in neatness, order, and comfort, always perfect. After dinner our boy slipped away to his old stool at my esteemed friend's knee, and there, with his hot chestnuts and his glass of brown sherry (really, a most excellent wine!) on a chair for a table, his face outshone the apples in the dish.

We talked of these jottings of mine, which Jemmy had read through and through by that time; and so it came about that my esteemed friend remarked, as she sat smoothing Jemmy's curls:

"And as you belong to the house too, Jemmy,--and so much more than the Lodgers, having been born in it,--why, your story ought to be added to the rest, I think, one of these days."

Jemmy's eyes sparkled at this, and he said, "So I think, Gran."

Then he sat looking at the fire, and then he began to laugh in a sort of confidence with the fire, and then he said, folding his arms across my esteemed friend's lap, and raising his bright face to hers. "Would you like to hear a boy's story, Gran?"

"Of all things," replied my esteemed friend.

"Would you, godfather?"

"Of all things," I too replied.

"Well, then," said Jemmy, "I'll tell you one."

Here our indisputably remarkable boy gave himself a hug, and laughed again, musically, at the idea of his coming out in that new line. Then he once more took the fire into the same sort of confidence as before, and began:

"Once upon a time, When pigs drank wine, And monkeys chewed tobaccer, 'Twas neither in your time nor mine, But that's no macker- -"

"Bless the child!" cried my esteemed friend, "what's amiss with his brain?"

"It's poetry, Gran," returned Jemmy, shouting with laughter. "We always begin stories that way at school."

"Gave me quite a turn, Major," said my esteemed friend, fanning herself with a plate. "Thought he was light-headed!"

"In those remarkable times, Gran and godfather, there was once a boy,--not me, you know."

"No, no," says my respected friend, "not you. Not him, Major, you understand?"

"No, no," says I.

"And he went to school in Rutlandshire--"

"Why not Lincolnshire?" says my respected friend.

"Why not, you dear old Gran? Because I go to school in Lincolnshire, don't I?"

"Ah, to be sure!" says my respected friend. "And it's not Jemmy, you understand, Major?"

"No, no," says I.

"Well!" our boy proceeded, hugging himself comfortably, and laughing merrily (again in confidence with the fire), before he again looked up in Mrs. Lirriper's face, "and so he was tremendously in love with his schoolmaster's daughter, and she was the most beautiful creature that ever was seen, and she had brown eyes, and she had brown hair all curling beautifully, and she had a delicious voice, and she was delicious altogether, and her name was Seraphina."

"What's the name of YOUR schoolmaster's daughter, Jemmy?" asks my respected friend.

"Polly!" replied Jemmy, pointing his forefinger at her. "There now! Caught you! Ha, ha, ha!"

When he and my respected friend had had a laugh and a hug together, our admittedly remarkable boy resumed with a great relish:

"Well! And so he loved her. And so he thought about her, and dreamed about her, and made her presents of oranges and nuts, and would have made her presents of pearls and diamonds if he could have afforded it out of his pocket-money, but he couldn't. And so her father--O, he WAS a Tartar! Keeping the boys up to the mark, holding examinations once a month, lecturing upon all sorts of subjects at all sorts of times, and knowing everything in the world out of book. And so this boy--"

"Had he any name?" asks my respected friend.

"No, he hadn't, Gran. Ha, ha! There now! Caught you again!"

After this, they had another laugh and another hug, and then our boy went on.

"Well! And so this boy, he had a friend about as old as himself at the same school, and his name (for He HAD a name, as it happened) was--let me remember--was Bobbo."

"Not Bob," says my respected friend.

"Of course not," says Jemmy. "What made you think it was, Gran? Well! And so this friend was the cleverest and bravest and best- looking and most generous of all the friends that ever were, and so he was in love with Seraphina's sister, and so Seraphina's sister was in love with him, and so they all grew up."

"Bless us!" says my respected friend. "They were very sudden about it."

"So they all grew up," our boy repeated, laughing heartily, "and Bobbo and this boy went away together on horseback to seek their fortunes, and they partly got their horses by favour, and partly in a bargain; that is to say, they had saved up between them seven and fourpence, and the two horses, being Arabs, were worth more, only the man said he would take that, to favour them. Well! And so they made their fortunes and came prancing back to the school, with their pockets full of gold, enough to last for ever. And so they rang at the parents' and visitors' bell (not the back gate), and when the bell was answered they proclaimed 'The same as if it was scarlet fever! Every boy goes home for an indefinite period!' And then there was great hurrahing, and then they kissed Seraphina and her sister,--each his own love, and not the other's on any account,--and then they ordered the Tartar into instant confinement."

"Poor man!" said my respected friend.

"Into instant confinement, Gran," repeated Jemmy, trying to look severe and roaring with laughter; "and he was to have nothing to eat but the boys' dinners, and was to drink half a cask of their beer every day. And so then the preparations were made for the two weddings, and there were hampers, and potted things, and sweet things, and nuts, and postage-stamps, and all manner of things. And so they were so jolly, that they let the Tartar out, and he was jolly too."

"I am glad they let him out," says my respected friend, "because he had only done his duty."

"O, but hadn't he overdone it, though!" cried Jemmy. "Well! And so then this boy mounted his horse, with his bride in his arms, and cantered away, and cantered on and on till he came to a certain place where he had a certain Gran and a certain godfather,--not you two, you know."

"No, no," we both said.

"And there he was received with great rejoicings, and he filled the cupboard and the bookcase with gold, and he showered it out on his Gran and his godfather because they were the two kindest and dearest people that ever lived in this world. And so while they were sitting up to their knees in gold, a knocking was heard at the street door, and who should it be but Bobbo, also on horseback with his bride in his arms, and what had he come to say but that he would take (at double rent) all the Lodgings for ever, that were not wanted by this a boy and this Gran and this godfather, and that they would all live together, and all be happy! And so they were, and so it never ended!"

"And was there no quarrelling?" asked my respected friend, as Jemmy sat upon her lap and hugged her.

"No! Nobody ever quarrelled."

"And did the money never melt away?"

"No! Nobody could ever spend it all."

"And did none of them ever grow older?"

"No! Nobody ever grew older after that."

"And did none of them ever die?"

"O, no, no, no, Gran!" exclaimed our dear boy, laying his cheek upon her breast, and drawing her closer to him. "Nobody ever died."

"Ah, Major, Major!" says my respected friend, smiling benignly upon me, "this beats our stories. Let us end with the Boy's story, Major, for the Boy's story is the best that is ever told!"

In submission to which request on the part of the best of women, I have here noted it down as faithfully as my best abilities, coupled with my best intentions, would admit, subscribing it with my name,

J. JACKMAN. THE PARLOURS. MRS. LIRRIPER'S LODGINGS.

Mrs Lirriper's Legacy

By Charles Dickens

CHAPTER I

MRS. LIRRIPER RELATES HOW SHE WENT ON, AND WENT OVER

Ah! It's pleasant to drop into my own easy-chair my dear though a little palpitating what with trotting up-stairs and what with trotting down, and why kitchen stairs should all be corner stairs is for the builders to justify though I do not think they fully understand their trade and never did, else why the sameness and why not more conveniences and fewer draughts and likewise making a practice of laying the plaster on too thick I am well convinced which holds the damp, and as to chimney-pots putting them on by guess-work like hats at a party and no more knowing what their effect will be upon the smoke bless you than I do if so much, except that it will mostly be either to send it down your throat in a straight form or give it a twist before it goes there. And what I says speaking as I find of those new metal chimneys all manner of shapes (there's a row of 'em at Miss Wozenham's lodging-house lower down on the other side of the way) is that they only work your smoke into artificial patterns for you before you swallow it and that I'd quite as soon swallow mine plain, the flavour being the same, not to mention the conceit of putting up signs on the top of your house to show the forms in which you take your smoke into your inside.

Being here before your eyes my dear in my own easy-chair in my own quiet room in my own Lodging-House Number Eighty-one Norfolk Street Strand London situated midway between the City and St. James's--if anything is where it used to be with these hotels calling themselves Limited but called unlimited by Major Jackman rising up everywhere and rising up into flagstaffs where they can't go any higher, but my mind of those monsters is give me a landlord's or landlady's wholesome face when I come off a journey and not a brass plate with an electrified number clicking out of it which it's not in nature can be glad to see me and to which I don't want to be hoisted like molasses at the Docks and left there telegraphing for help with the most ingenious instruments but quite in vain--being here my dear I have no call to mention that I am still in the Lodgings as a business hoping to die in the same and if agreeable to the clergy partly read over at Saint Clement's Danes and concluded in Hatfield churchyard when lying once again by my poor Lirriper ashes to ashes and dust to dust.

Neither should I tell you any news my dear in telling you that the Major is still a fixture in the Parlours quite as much so as the roof of the house, and that Jemmy is of boys the best and brightest and has ever had kept from him the cruel story of his poor pretty young mother Mrs. Edson being deserted in the second floor and dying in my arms, fully believing that I am his born Gran and him an orphan, though what with engineering since he took a taste for it and him and the Major making Locomotives out of parasols broken iron pots and cotton-reels and them absolutely a getting off the line and falling over the table and injuring the passengers almost equal to the originals it really is quite wonderful. And when I says to the Major, "Major can't you by ANY means give us a communication with the guard?" the Major says quite huffy, "No madam it's not to be done," and when I says "Why not?" the Major says, "That is between us who are in the Railway Interest madam and our friend the Right Honourable Vice-President of the Board of Trade" and if you'll believe me my dear the Major wrote to Jemmy at school to consult him on the answer I should have before I could get even that amount of unsatisfactoriness out of the man, the reason being that when we first began with the little model and the working signals beautiful and perfect (being in general as wrong as the real) and when I says laughing "What appointment am I to hold in this undertaking gentlemen?" Jemmy hugs me round the neck and tells me dancing, "You shall be the Public Gran" and consequently they put upon me just as much as ever they like and I sit a growling in my easy-chair.

My dear whether it is that a grown man as clever as the Major cannot give half his heart and mind to anything--even a plaything--but must get into right down earnest with it, whether it is so or whether it is not so I do not undertake to say, but Jemmy is far out-done by the serious and believing ways of the Major in the management of the United Grand Junction Lirriper and Jackman Great Norfolk Parlour Line, "For" says my Jemmy with the sparkling eyes when it was christened, "we must have a whole mouthful of name Gran or our dear old Public" and there the young rogue kissed me, "won't stump up." So the Public took the shares--ten at ninepence, and immediately when that was spent twelve Preference at one and sixpence--

and they were all signed by Jemmy and countersigned by the Major, and between ourselves much better worth the money than some shares I have paid for in my time. In the same holidays the line was made and worked and opened and ran excursions and had collisions and burst its boilers and all sorts of accidents and offences all most regular correct and pretty. The sense of responsibility entertained by the Major as a military style of station-master my dear starting the down train behind time and ringing one of those little bells that you buy with the little coal-scuttles off the tray round the man's neck in the street did him honour, but noticing the Major of a night when he is writing out his monthly report to Jemmy at school of the state of the Rolling Stock and the Permanent Way and all the rest of it (the whole kept upon the Major's sideboard and dusted with his own hands every morning before varnishing his boots) I notice him as full of thought and care as full can be and frowning in a fearful manner, but indeed the Major does nothing by halves as witness his great delight in going out surveying with Jemmy when he has Jemmy to go with, carrying a chain and a measuring-tape and driving I don't know what improvements right through Westminster Abbey and fully believed in the streets to be knocking everything upside down by Act of Parliament. As please Heaven will come to pass when Jemmy takes to that as a profession!

Mentioning my poor Lirriper brings into my head his own youngest brother the Doctor though Doctor of what I am sure it would be hard to say unless Liquor, for neither Physic nor Music nor yet Law does Joshua Lirriper know a morsel of except continually being summoned to the County Court and having orders made upon him which he runs away from, and once was taken in the passage of this very house with an umbrella up and the Major's hat on, giving his name with the door-mat round him as Sir Johnson Jones, K.C.B. in spectacles residing at the Horse Guards. On which occasion he had got into the house not a minute before, through the girl letting him on the mat when he sent in a piece of paper twisted more like one of those spills for lighting candles than a note, offering me the choice between thirty shillings in hand and his brains on the premises marked immediate and waiting for an answer. My dear it gave me such a dreadful turn to think of the brains of my poor dear Lirriper's own flesh and blood flying about the new oilcloth however unworthy to be so assisted, that I went out of my room here to ask him what he would take once for all not to do it for life when I found him in the custody of two gentlemen that I should have judged to be in the feather-bed trade if they had not announced the law, so fluffy were their personal appearance. "Bring your chains, sir," says Joshua to the littlest of the two in the biggest hat, "rivet on my fetters!" Imagine my feelings when I pictered him clanking up Norfolk Street in irons and Miss Wozenham looking out of window! "Gentlemen," I says all of a tremble and ready to drop "please to bring him into Major Jackman's apartments." So they brought him into the Parlours, and when the Major spies his own curly-brimmed hat on him which Joshua Lirriper had whipped off its peg in the passage for a military disguise he goes into such a tearing passion that he tips it off his head with his hand and kicks it up to the ceiling with his foot where it grazed long afterwards. "Major" I says "be cool and advise me what to do with Joshua my dead and gone Lirriper's own youngest brother." "Madam" says the Major "my advice is that you board and lodge him in a Powder Mill, with a handsome gratuity to the proprietor when exploded." "Major" I says "as a Christian you cannot mean your words." "Madam" says the Major "by the Lord I do!" and indeed the Major besides being with all his merits a very passionate man for his size had a bad opinion of Joshua on account of former troubles even unattended by liberties taken with his apparel. When Joshua Lirriper hears this conversation betwixt us he turns upon the littlest one with the biggest hat and says "Come sir! Remove me to my vile dungeon. Where is my mouldy straw?" My dear at the picter of him rising in my mind dressed almost entirely in padlocks like Baron Trenck in Jemmy's book I was so overcome that I burst into tears and I says to the Major, "Major take my keys and settle with these gentlemen or I shall never know a happy minute more," which was done several times both before and since, but still I must remember that Joshua Lirriper has his good feelings and shows them in being always so troubled in his mind when he cannot wear mourning for his brother. Many a long year have I left off my widow's mourning not being wishful to intrude, but the tender point in Joshua that I cannot help a little yielding to is when he writes "One single sovereign would enable me to wear a decent suit of mourning for my much-loved brother. I vowed at the time of his lamented death that I would ever wear sables in memory of him but Alas how short-sighted is man, How keep that vow when penniless!" It says a good deal for the strength of his feelings that he couldn't have been seven year old when my poor Lirriper died and to have kept to it ever since is highly creditable. But we know there's good in all of us,--if we only knew where it was in some of us,--and though it was far from delicate in Joshua to work upon the dear child's feelings when first sent to school and write down into Lincolnshire for his pocket-money by return of post and got it, still he is my poor Lirriper's own youngest brother and mightn't have meant not paying his bill at the Salisbury Arms when his affection took him down to stay a fortnight at Hatfield churchyard and might have meant to keep sober but for bad company. Consequently if the Major HAD played on him with the garden-engine which he got privately into his room without my knowing of it, I think that much as I should have regretted it there would have been words betwixt the Major and me. Therefore my dear though he played on Mr. Buffle by mistake being hot in his head, and though it might have been misrepresented down at Wozenham's into not being ready for Mr. Buffle in other respects he being the Assessed Taxes, still I do not so much regret it as perhaps I ought. And whether Joshua Lirriper will yet do well in life I cannot say, but I did hear of his coming, out at a Private Theatre in the character of a Bandit without receiving any offers afterwards from the regular managers.

Mentioning Mr. Baffle gives an instance of there being good in persons where good is not expected, for it cannot be denied that Mr. Buffle's manners when engaged in his business were not agreeable. To collect is one thing, and to look about as if suspicious of the goods being gradually removing in the dead of the night by a back door is another, over taxing you have no control but suspecting is voluntary. Allowances too must ever be made for a gentleman of the Major's warmth not relishing being spoke to with a pen in the mouth, and while I do not know that it is more irritable to my own feelings to have a low-crowned hat with a broad brim kept on in doors than any other hat still I can appreciate the Major's, besides which without bearing malice or vengeance the Major is a man that scores up arrears as his habit always was with Joshua Lirriper. So at last my dear the Major lay in wait for Mr. Buffle, and it worrited me a good deal. Mr. Buffle gives his rap of two sharp knocks one day and the Major bounces to the door. "Collector has called for two quarters' Assessed Taxes" says Mr. Buffle. "They are ready for him" says the Major and brings him in here. But on the way Mr. Buffle looks about him in his usual suspicious manner and the Major fires and asks him "Do you see a Ghost sir?" "No sir" says Mr. Buffle. "Because I have before noticed you" says the Major "apparently looking for a spectre very hard beneath the roof of my respected friend. When you find that supernatural agent, be so good as point him out sir." Mr. Buffle stares at the Major and then nods at me. "Mrs. Lirriper sir" says the Major going off into a perfect steam and introducing me with his hand. "Pleasure of knowing her" says Mr. Buffle. "A--hum!--Jemmy Jackman sir!" says the Major introducing himself. "Honour of knowing you by sight" says Mr. Buffle. "Jemmy Jackman sir" says the Major wagging his head sideways in a sort of obstinate fury "presents to you his esteemed friend that lady Mrs. Emma Lirriper of Eighty-one Norfolk Street Strand London in the County of Middlesex in the United Kingdom of Great Britain and Ireland. Upon which occasion sir," says the Major, "Jemmy Jackman takes your hat off." Mr. Buffle looks at his hat where the Major drops it on the floor, and he picks it up and puts it on again. "Sir" says the Major very red and looking him full in the face "there are two quarters of the Gallantry Taxes due and the Collector has called." Upon which if you can believe my words my dear the Major drops Mr. Buffle's hat off again. "This--" Mr. Buffle begins very angry with his pen in his mouth, when the Major steaming more and more says "Take your bit out sir! Or by the whole infernal system of Taxation of this country and every individual figure in the National Debt, I'll get upon your back and ride you like a horse!" which it's my belief he would have done and even actually jerking his neat little legs ready for a spring as it was. "This," says Mr. Buffle without his pen "is an assault and I'll have the law of you." "Sir" replies the Major "if you are a man of honour, your Collector of whatever may be due on the Honourable Assessment by applying to Major Jackman at the Parlours Mrs. Lirriper's Lodgings, may obtain what he wants in full at any moment."

When the Major glared at Mr. Buffle with those meaning words my dear I literally gasped for a teaspoonful of salvolatile in a wine-glass of water, and I says "Pray let it go no farther gentlemen I beg and beseech of you!" But the Major could be got to do nothing else but snort long after Mr. Buffle was gone, and the effect it had upon my whole mass of blood when on the next day of Mr. Buffle's rounds the Major spruced himself up and went humming a tune up and down the street with one eye almost obliterated by his hat there are not expressions in Johnson's Dictionary to state. But I safely put the street door on the jar and got behind the Major's blinds with my shawl on and my mind made up the moment I saw danger to rush out screeching till my voice failed me and catch the Major round the neck till my strength went and have all parties bound. I had not been behind the blinds a quarter of an hour when I saw Mr. Buffle approaching with his Collecting-books in his hand. The Major likewise saw him approaching and hummed louder and himself approached. They met before the Airy railings. The Major takes off his hat at arm's length and says "Mr. Buffle I believe?" Mr. Buffle takes off HIS hat at arm's length and says "That is my name sir." Says the Major "Have you any commands for me, Mr. Buffle?" Says Mr. Buffle "Not any sir." Then my dear both of 'em bowed very low and haughty and parted, and whenever Mr. Buffle made his rounds in future him and the Major always met and bowed before the Airy railings, putting me much in mind of Hamlet and the other gentleman in mourning before killing one another, though I could have wished the other gentleman had done it fairer and even if less polite no poison.

Mr. Buffle's family were not liked in this neighbourhood, for when you are a householder my dear you'll find it does not come by nature to like the Assessed, and it was considered besides that a one-horse pheayton ought not to have elevated Mrs. Buffle to that height especially when purloined from the Taxes which I myself did consider uncharitable. But they were NOT liked and there was that domestic unhappiness in the family in consequence of their both being very hard with Miss Buffle and one another on account of Miss Buffle's favouring Mr. Buffle's articled young gentleman, that it WAS whispered that Miss Buffle would go either into a consumption or a convent she being so very thin and off her appetite and two close- shaved gentlemen with white bands round their necks peeping round the corner whenever she went out in waistcoats resembling black pinafores. So things stood towards Mr. Buffle when one night I was woke by a frightful noise and a smell of burning, and going to my bedroom window saw the whole street in a glow. Fortunately we had two sets empty just then and before I could hurry on some clothes I heard the Major hammering at the attics' doors and calling out "Dress yourselves!--Fire! Don't be frightened!--Fire! Collect your presence of mind!--Fire! All right--Fire!" most tremenjously. As I opened my bedroom door the Major came tumbling in over himself and me, and caught me in his arms. "Major" I says breathless "where is it?" "I don't know dearest madam" says the Major--"Fire! Jemmy Jackman will defend you to the last drop of his blood--Fire! If the dear boy was at home what a treat this would be for him--Fire!" and altogether very collected and bold except that he couldn't say a single sentence without shaking me to the very centre with roaring Fire. We ran down to the drawing-room and put our heads out of window, and the Major calls to an unfeeling young monkey, scampering by be joyful and ready to split "Where is it?--Fire!" The monkey answers without stopping "O here's a lark! Old Buffle's been setting his house alight to prevent its being found out that he boned the Taxes. Hurrah! Fire!" And then the sparks came flying up and the smoke came pouring down and the crackling of flames and spatting of water and banging of engines and hacking of axes and breaking of glass and knocking at doors and the shouting and crying and hurrying and the heat and altogether gave me a dreadful palpitation. "Don't be frightened dearest madam," says the Major, "--Fire! There's nothing to be alarmed at--Fire! Don't open the street door till I come back--Fire! I'll go and see if I can be of any service--Fire! You're quite composed and comfortable ain't you?--Fire, Fire, Fire!" It was in vain for me to hold the man and tell him he'd be galloped to death by the engines--pumped to death by his over-exertions--wet-feeted to death by the slop and mess-- flattened to death when the roofs fell in--his spirit was up and he went scampering off after the young monkey with all the breath he had and none to spare, and me and the girls huddled together at the parlour windows looking at the dreadful flames above the houses over the way, Mr. Buffle's being round the corner. Presently what should we see but some people running down the street straight to our door, and then the

Major directing operations in the busiest way, and then some more people and then--carried in a chair similar to Guy Fawkes- -Mr. Buffle in a blanket!

My dear the Major has Mr. Buffle brought up our steps and whisked into the parlour and carted out on the sofy, and then he and all the rest of them without so much as a word burst away again full speed leaving the impression of a vision except for Mr. Buffle awful in his blanket with his eyes a rolling. In a twinkling they all burst back again with Mrs. Buffle in another blanket, which whisked in and carted out on the sofy they all burst off again and all burst back again with Miss Buffle in another blanket, which again whisked in and carted out they all burst off again and all burst back again with Mr. Buffle's articled young gentleman in another blanket--him a holding round the necks of two men carrying him by the legs, similar to the picter of the disgraceful creetur who has lost the fight (but where the chair I do not know) and his hair having the appearance of newly played upon. When all four of a row, the Major rubs his hands and whispers me with what little hoarseness he can get together, "If our dear remarkable boy was only at home what a delightful treat this would be for him!"

My dear we made them some hot tea and toast and some hot brandy-and-water with a little comfortable nutmeg in it, and at first they were scared and low in their spirits but being fully insured got sociable. And the first use Mr. Buffle made of his tongue was to call the Major his Preserver and his best of friends and to say "My for ever dearest sir let me make you known to Mrs. Buffle" which also addressed him as her Preserver and her best of friends and was fully as cordial as the blanket would admit of. Also Miss Buffle. The articled young gentleman's head was a little light and he sat a moaning "Robina is reduced to cinders, Robina is reduced to cinders!" Which went more to the heart on account of his having got wrapped in his blanket as if he was looking out of a violinceller case, until Mr. Buffle says "Robina speak to him!" Miss Buffle says "Dear George!" and but for the Major's pouring down brandy-and-water on the instant which caused a catching in his throat owing to the nutmeg and a violent fit of coughing it might have proved too much for his strength. When the articled young gentleman got the better of it Mr.

Buffle leaned up against Mrs. Buffle being two bundles, a little while in confidence, and then says with tears in his eyes which the Major noticing wiped, "We have not been an united family, let us after this danger become so, take her George." The young gentleman could not put his arm out far to do it, but his spoken expressions were very beautiful though of a wandering class. And I do not know that I ever had a much pleasanter meal than the breakfast we took together after we had all dozed, when Miss Buffle made tea very sweetly in quite the Roman style as depicted formerly at Covent Garden Theatre and when the whole family was most agreeable, as they have ever proved since that night when the Major stood at the foot of the Fire-Escape and claimed them as they came down--the young gentleman head-foremost, which accounts. And though I do not say that we should be less liable to think ill of one another if strictly limited to blankets, still I do say that we might most of us come to a better understanding if we kept one another less at a distance.

Why there's Wozenham's lower down on the other side of the street. I had a feeling of much soreness several years respecting what I must still ever call Miss Wozenham's systematic underbidding and the likeness of the house in Bradshaw having far too many windows and a most umbrageous and outrageous Oak which never yet was seen in Norfolk Street nor yet a carriage and four at Wozenham's door, which it would have been far more to Bradshaw's credit to have drawn a cab. This frame of mind continued bitter down to the very afternoon in January last when one of my girls, Sally Rairyganoo which I still suspect of Irish extraction though family represented Cambridge, else why abscond with a bricklayer of the Limerick persuasion and be married in pattens not waiting till his black eye was decently got round with all the company fourteen in number and one horse fighting outside on the roof of the vehicle,--I repeat my dear my ill- regulated state of mind towards Miss Wozenham continued down to the very afternoon of January last past when Sally Rairyganoo came banging (I can use no milder expression) into my room with a jump which may be Cambridge and may not, and said "Hurroo Missis! Miss Wozenham's sold up!" My dear when I had it thrown in my face and conscience that the girl Sally had reason to think I could be glad of the ruin of a fellow-creeter, I burst into tears and dropped back in my chair and I says "I am ashamed of myself!"

Well! I tried to settle to my tea but I could not do it what with thinking of Miss Wozenham and her distresses. It was a wretched night and I went up to a front window and looked over at Wozenham's and as well as I could make it out down the street in the fog it was the dismallest of the dismal and not a light to be seen. So at last I says to myself "This will not do," and I puts on my oldest bonnet and shawl not wishing Miss Wozenham to be reminded of my best at such a time, and lo and behold you I goes over to Wozenham's and knocks. "Miss Wozenham at home?" I says turning my head when I heard the door go. And then I saw it was Miss Wozenham herself who had opened it and sadly worn she was poor thing and her eyes all swelled and swelled with crying. "Miss Wozenham" I says "it is several years since there was a little unpleasantness betwixt us on the subject of my grandson's cap being down your Airy. I have overlooked it and I hope you have done the same." "Yes Mrs. Lirriper" she says in a surprise, I have." "Then my dear" I says "I should be glad to come in and speak a word to you." Upon my calling her my dear Miss Wozenham breaks out a crying most pitiful, and a not unfeeling elderly person that might have been better shaved in a nightcap with a hat over it offering a polite apology for the mumps having worked themselves into his constitution, and also for sending home to his wife on the bellows which was in his hand as a writing-desk, looks out of the back parlour and says "The lady wants a word of comfort" and goes in again. So I was able to say quite natural "Wants a word of comfort does she sir? Then please the pigs she shall have it!" And Miss Wozenham and me we go into the front room with a wretched light that seemed to have been crying too and was sputtering out, and I says "Now my dear, tell me all," and she wrings her hands and says "O Mrs. Lirriper that man is in possession here, and I have not a friend in the world who is able to help me with a shilling."

It doesn't signify a bit what a talkative old body like me said to Miss Wozenham when she said that, and so I'll tell you instead my dear that I'd have given thirty shillings to have taken her over to tea, only I durstn't on account of the Major. Not you see but what I knew I could draw the Major out like thread and wind him round my finger on most subjects and perhaps even on that if I was to set myself to it, but him and me had so often belied Miss Wozenham to one another that I was shamefaced, and I knew she had offended his pride and never mine, and likewise I felt timid that that Rairyganoo girl might make things awkward. So I says "My dear if you could give me a cup of tea to clear my muddle of a head I should better understand your affairs." And we had the tea and the affairs too and after all it was but forty pound, and--There! she's as industrious and straight a creeter as ever lived and has paid back half of it already, and where's the use of saying more, particularly when it ain't the point? For the point is that when she was a kissing my hands and holding them in hers and kissing them again and blessing blessing blessing, I cheered up at last and I says "Why what a waddling old goose I have been my dear to take you for something so very different!" "Ah but I too" says she "how have I mistaken YOU!" "Come for goodness' sake tell me" I says "what you thought of me?" "O" says she "I thought you had no feeling for such a hard hand-to-mouth life as mine, and were rolling in affluence." I says shaking my sides (and very glad to do it for I had been a choking quite long enough) "Only look at my figure my dear and give me your opinion whether if I was in affluence I should be likely to roll in it? "That did it? We got as merry as grigs (whatever THEY are, if you happen to know my dear--I don't) and I went home to my blessed home as happy and as thankful as could be. But before I make an end of it, think even of my having misunderstood the Major! Yes! For next forenoon the Major came into my little room with his brushed hat in his hand and he begins "My dearest madam--" and then put his face in his hat as if he had just come into church. As I sat all in a maze he came out of his hat and began again. "My esteemed and beloved friend--" and then went into his hat again. "Major," I cries out frightened "has anything happened to our darling boy?" "No, no, no" says the Major "but Miss Wozenham has been here this morning to make her excuses to me, and by the Lord I can't get over what she told me." "Hoity toity, Major," I says "you don't know yet that I was afraid of you last night and didn't think half as well of you as I ought! So come out of church Major and forgive me like a dear old friend and I'll never do so any more." And I leave you to judge my dear whether I ever did or will. And how affecting to think of Miss Wozenham out of her small income and her losses doing so much for her poor old father, and keeping a brother that had had the misfortune to soften his brain against the hard mathematics as neat as a new pin in the three back represented to lodgers as a lumber-room and consuming a whole shoulder of mutton whenever provided!

And now my dear I really am a going to tell you about my Legacy if you're inclined to favour me with your attention, and I did fully intend to have come straight to it only one thing does so bring up another. It was the month of June and the day before Midsummer Day when my girl Winifred Madgers-- she was what is termed a Plymouth Sister, and the Plymouth Brother that made away with her was quite right, for a tidier young woman for a wife never came into a house and afterwards called with the beautifullest Plymouth Twins--it was the day before Midsummer Day when Winifred Madgers comes and says to me "A gentleman from the Consul's wishes particular to speak to Mrs. Lirriper." If you'll believe me my dear the Consols at the bank where I have a little matter for Jemmy got into my head, and I says "Good gracious I hope he ain't had any dreadful fall!" Says Winifred "He don't look as if he had ma'am." And I says "Show him in."

The gentleman came in dark and with his hair cropped what I should consider too close, and he says very polite "Madame Lirrwiper!" I says, "Yes sir. Take a chair." "I come," says he "frrwom the Frrwench Consul's." So I saw at once that it wasn't the Bank of England. "We have rrweceived," says the gentleman turning his r's very curious and skilful, "frrwom the Mairrwie at Sens, a communication which I will have the honour to rrwead. Madame Lirrwiper understands Frrwench?" "O dear no sir!" says I. "Madame Lirriper don't understand anything of the sort." "It matters not," says the gentleman, "I will trrwanslate."

With that my dear the gentleman after reading something about a Department and a Marie (which Lord forgive me I supposed till the Major came home was Mary, and never was I more puzzled than to think how that young woman came to have so much to do with it) translated a lot with the most obliging pains, and it came to this:- That in the town of Sons in France an unknown Englishman lay a dying. That he was speechless and without motion. That in his lodging there was a gold watch and a purse containing such and such money and a trunk containing such and such clothes, but no passport and no papers, except that on his table was a pack of cards and that he had written in pencil on the back of the ace of hearts: "To the authorities. When I am dead, pray send what is left, as a last Legacy, to Mrs. Lirriper Eighty-one Norfolk Street Strand London." When the gentleman had explained all this, which seemed to be drawn up much more methodical than I should have given the French credit for, not at that time knowing the nation, he put the document into my hand. And much the wiser I was for that you may be sure, except that it had the look of being made out upon grocery paper and was stamped all over with eagles.

"Does Madame Lirrwiper" says the gentleman "believe she rrwecognises her unfortunate compatrrwiot?"

You may imagine the flurry it put me into my dear to he talked to about my compatriots.

I says "Excuse me. Would you have the kindness sir to make your language as simple as you can?"

"This Englishman unhappy, at the point of death. This compatrrwiot afflicted," says the gentleman.

"Thank you sir" I says "I understand you now. No sir I have not the least idea who this can be."

"Has Madame Lirrwiper no son, no nephew, no godson, no frrwiend, no acquaintance of any kind in Frrwance?"

"To my certain knowledge" says I "no relation or friend, and to the best of my belief no acquaintance."

"Pardon me. You take Locataires?" says the gentleman.

My dear fully believing he was offering me something with his obliging foreign manners,-- snuff for anything I knew,--I gave a little bend of my head and I says if you'll credit it, "No I thank you. I have not contracted the habit."

The gentleman looks perplexed and says "Lodgers!"

"Oh!" says I laughing. "Bless the man! Why yes to be sure!"

"May it not be a former lodger?" says the gentleman. "Some lodger that you pardoned some rrwent? You have pardoned lodgers some rrwent?"

"Hem! It has happened sir" says I, "but I assure you I can call to mind no gentleman of that description that this is at all likely to be."

In short my dear, we could make nothing of it, and the gentleman noted down what I said and went away. But he left me the paper of which he had two with him, and when the Major came in I says to the Major as I put it in his hand "Major here's Old Moore's Almanac with the hieroglyphic complete, for your opinion."

It took the Major a little longer to read than I should have thought, judging from the copious flow with which he seemed to be gifted when attacking the organ-men, but at last he got through it, and stood a gazing at me in amazement.

"Major" I says "you're paralysed."

"Madam" says the Major, "Jemmy Jackman is doubled up."

Now it did so happen that the Major had been out to get a little information about railroads and steamboats, as our boy was coming home for his Midsummer holidays next day and we were going to take him somewhere for a treat and a change. So while the Major stood a gazing it came into my head to say to him "Major I wish you'd go and look at some of your books and maps, and see whereabouts this same town of Sens is in France."

The Major he roused himself and he went into the Parlours and he poked about a little, and he came back to me and he says, "Sens my dearest madam is seventy-odd miles south of Paris."

With what I may truly call a desperate effort "Major," I says "we'll go there with our blessed boy."

If ever the Major was beside himself it was at the thoughts of that journey. All day long he was like the wild man of the woods after meeting with an advertisement in the papers telling him something to his advantage, and early next morning hours before Jemmy could possibly come home he was outside in the street ready to call out to him that we was all a going to France. Young Rosycheeks you may believe was as wild as the Major, and they did carry on to that degree that I says "If you two children ain't more orderly I'll pack you both off to bed." And then they fell to cleaning up the Major's telescope to see France with, and went out and bought a leather bag with a snap to hang round Jemmy, and him to carry the money like a little Fortunatus with his purse.

If I hadn't passed my word and raised their hopes, I doubt if I could have gone through with the undertaking but it was too late to go back now. So on the second day after Midsummer Day we went off by the morning mail. And when we came to the sea which I had never seen but once in my life and that when my poor Lirriper was courting me, the freshness of it and the deepness and the airiness and to think that it had been rolling ever since and that it was always a rolling and so few of us minding, made me feel quite serious. But I felt happy too and so did Jemmy and the Major and not much motion on the whole, though me with a swimming in the head and a sinking but able to take notice that the foreign insides appear to be constructed hollower than the English, leading to much more tremenjous noises when bad sailors.

But my dear the blueness and the lightness and the coloured look of everything and the very sentry-boxes striped and the shining rattling drums and the little soldiers with their waists and tidy gaiters, when we got across to the Continent--it made me feel as if I don't know what--as if the atmosphere had been lifted off me. And as to lunch why bless you if I kept a man-cook and two kitchen-maids I couldn't got it done for twice the money, and no injured young woman a glaring at you and grudging you and acknowledging your patronage by wishing that your food might choke you, but so civil and so hot and attentive and every way comfortable except Jemmy pouring wine down his throat by tumblers-full and me expecting to see him drop under the table.

And the way in which Jemmy spoke his French was a real charm. It was often wanted of him, for whenever anybody spoke a syllable to me I says "Non-comprenny, you're very kind, but it's no use--Now Jemmy!" and then Jemmy he fires away at 'em lovely, the only thing wanting in Jemmy's French being as it appeared to me that he hardly ever understood a word of what they said to him which made it scarcely of the use it might have been though in other respects a perfect Native, and regarding the Major's fluency I should have been of the opinion judging French by English that there might have been a greater choice of words in the language though still I must admit that if I hadn't known him when he asked a military gentleman in a gray cloak what o'clock it was I should have took him for a Frenchman born.

Before going on to look after my Legacy we were to make one regular day in Paris, and I leave you to judge my dear what a day THAT was with Jemmy and the Major and the telescope and me and the prowling young man at the inn door (but very civil too) that went along with us to show the sights. All along the railway to Paris Jemmy and the Major had been frightening me to death by stooping down on the platforms at stations to inspect the engines underneath their mechanical stomachs, and by creeping in and out I don't know where all, to find improvements for the United Grand Junction Parlour, but when we got out into the brilliant streets on a bright morning they gave up all their London improvements as a bad job and gave their minds to Paris. Says the prowling young man to me "Will I speak Inglis No?" So I says "If you can young man I shall take it as a favour," but after half-an-hour of it when I fully believed the man had gone mad and me too I says "Be so good as fall back on your French sir," knowing that then I shouldn't have the agonies of trying to understand him, which was a happy release. Not that I lost much more than the rest either, for I generally noticed that when he had described something very long indeed and I says to Jemmy "What does he say Jemmy?" Jemmy says looking with vengeance in his eye "He is so jolly indistinct!" and that when he had described it longer all over again and I says to Jemmy "Well Jemmy what's it all about?" Jemmy says "He says the building was repaired in seventeen hundred and four, Gran."

Wherever that prowling young man formed his prowling habits I cannot be expected to know, but the way in which he went round the corner while we had our breakfasts and was there again when we swallowed the last crumb was most marvellous, and just the same at dinner and at night, prowling equally at the theatre and the inn gateway and the shop doors when we bought a trifle or two and everywhere else but troubled with a tendency to spit. And of Paris I can tell you no more my dear than that it's town and country both in one, and carved stone and long streets of high houses and gardens and fountains and statues and trees and gold, and immensely big soldiers and immensely little soldiers and the pleasantest nurses with the whitest caps a playing at skipping-rope with the bunchiest babies in the flattest caps, and clean table-cloths spread everywhere for dinner and people sitting out of doors smoking and sipping all day long and little plays being acted in the open air for little people and every shop a complete and elegant room, and everybody seeming to play at everything in this world. And as to the sparkling lights my dear after dark, glittering high up and low down and on before and on behind and all round, and the crowd of theatres and the crowd of people and the crowd of all sorts, it's pure enchantment. And pretty well the only thing that grated on me was that whether you pay your fare at the railway or whether you change your money at a money-dealer's or whether you take your ticket at the theatre, the lady or gentleman is caged up (I suppose by government) behind the strongest iron bars having more of a Zoological appearance than a free country.

Well to be sure when I did after all get my precious bones to bed that night, and my Young Rogue came in to kiss me and asks "What do you think of this lovely lovely Paris, Gran?" I says "Jemmy I feel as if it was beautiful fireworks being let off in my head." And very cool and refreshing the pleasant country was next day when we went on to look after my Legacy, and rested me much and did me a deal of good.

So at length and at last my dear we come to Sens, a pretty little town with a great two-towered cathedral and the rooks flying in and out of the loopholes and another tower atop of one of the towers like a sort of a stone pulpit. In which pulpit with the birds skimming below him if you'll believe me, I saw a speck while I was resting at the inn before dinner which they made signs to me was Jemmy and which really was. I had been a fancying as I sat in the balcony of the hotel that an Angel might light there and call down to the people to be good, but I little thought what Jemmy all unknown to himself was a calling down from that high place to some one in the town.

The pleasantest-situated inn my dear! Right under the two towers, with their shadows a changing upon it all day like a kind of a sundial, and country people driving in and out of the courtyard in carts and hooded cabriolets and such like, and a market outside in front of the cathedral, and all so quaint and like a picter. The Major and me agreed that whatever came of my Legacy this was the place to stay in for our holiday, and we also agreed that our dear boy had best not be checked in his joy that night by the sight of the Englishman if he was still alive, but that we would go together and alone. For you are to understand that the Major not feeling himself quite equal in his wind to the height to which Jemmy had climbed, had come back to me and left him with the Guide.

So after dinner when Jemmy had set off to see the river, the Major went down to the Mairie, and presently came back with a military character in a sword and spurs and a cocked hat and a yellow shoulder-belt and long tags about him that he must have found inconvenient. And the Major says "The Englishman still lies in the same state dearest madam. This gentleman will conduct us to his lodging." Upon which the military character pulled off his cocked hat to me, and I took notice that he had shaved his forehead in imitation of Napoleon Bonaparte but not like.

We wont out at the courtyard gate and past the great doors of the cathedral and down a narrow High Street where the people were sitting chatting at their shop doors and the children were at play. The military character went in front and he stopped at a pork-shop with a little statue of a pig sitting up, in the window, and a private door that a donkey was looking out of.

When the donkey saw the military character he came slipping out on the pavement to turn round and then clattered along the passage into a back yard. So the coast being clear, the Major and me were conducted up the common stair and into the front room on the second, a bare room with a red tiled floor and the outside lattice blinds pulled close to darken it. As the military character opened the blinds I saw the tower where I had seen Jemmy, darkening as the sun got low, and I turned to the bed by the wall and saw the Englishman.

It was some kind of brain fever he had had, and his hair was all gone, and some wetted folded linen lay upon his head. I looked at him very attentive as he lay there all wasted away with his eyes closed, and I says to the Major

"I never saw this face before."

The Major looked at him very attentive too, and he says "I never saw this face before."

When the Major explained our words to the military character, that gentleman shrugged his shoulders and showed the Major the card on which it was written about the Legacy for me. It had been written with a weak and trembling hand in bed, and I knew no more of the writing than of the face. Neither did the Major.

Though lying there alone, the poor creetur was as well taken care of as could be hoped, and would have been quite unconscious of any one's sitting by him then. I got the Major to say that we were not going away at present and that I would come back to-morrow and watch a bit by the bedside. But I got him to add--and I shook my head hard to make it stronger--"We agree that we never saw this face before."

Our boy was greatly surprised when we told him sitting out in the balcony in the starlight, and he ran over some of those stories of former Lodgers, of the Major's putting down, and asked wasn't it possible that it might be this lodger or that lodger. It was not possible, and we went to bed.

In the morning just at breakfast-time the military character came jingling round, and said that the doctor thought from the signs he saw there might be some rally before the end. So I says to the Major and Jemmy, "You two boys go and enjoy yourselves, and I'll take my Prayer Book and go sit by the bed." So I went, and I sat there some hours, reading a prayer for him poor soul now and then, and it was quite on in the day when he moved his hand.

He had been so still, that the moment he moved I knew of it, and I pulled off my spectacles and laid down my book and rose and looked at him. From moving one hand he began to move both, and then his action was the action of a person groping in the dark. Long after his eyes had opened, there was a film over them and he still felt for his way out into light. But by slow degrees his sight cleared and his hands stopped. He saw the ceiling, he saw the wall, he saw me. As his sight cleared, mine cleared too, and when at last we looked in one another's faces, I started back, and I cries passionately:

"O you wicked wicked man! Your sin has found you out!"

For I knew him, the moment life looked out of his eyes, to be Mr. Edson, Jemmy's father who had so cruelly deserted Jemmy's young unmarried mother who had died in my arms, poor tender creetur, and left Jemmy to me.

"You cruel wicked man! You bad black traitor!"

With the little strength he had, he made an attempt to turn over on his wretched face to hide it. His arm dropped out of the bed and his head with it, and there he lay before me crushed in body and in mind. Surely the miserablest sight under the summer sun!

"O blessed Heaven," I says a crying, "teach me what to say to this broken mortal! I am a poor sinful creetur, and the Judgment is not mine."

As I lifted my eyes up to the clear bright sky, I saw the high tower where Jemmy had stood above the birds, seeing that very window; and the last look of that poor pretty young mother when her soul brightened and got free, seemed to shine down from it.

"O man, man, man!" I says, and I went on my knees beside the bed; "if your heart is rent asunder and you are truly penitent for what you did, Our Saviour will have mercy on you yet!"

As I leaned my face against the bed, his feeble hand could just move itself enough to touch me. I hope the touch was penitent. It tried to hold my dress and keep hold, but the fingers were too weak to close.

I lifted him back upon the pillows and I says to him:

"Can you hear me?"

He looked yes.

"Do you know me?"

He looked yes, even yet more plainly.

"I am not here alone. The Major is with me. You recollect the Major?"

Yes. That is to say he made out yes, in the same way as before.

"And even the Major and I are not alone. My grandson--his godson-- is with us. Do you hear? My grandson."

The fingers made another trial to catch my sleeve, but could only creep near it and fall.

"Do you know who my grandson is?"

Yes.

"I pitied and loved his lonely mother. When his mother lay a dying I said to her, 'My dear, this baby is sent to a childless old woman.' He has been my pride and joy ever since. I love him as dearly as if he had drunk from my breast. Do you ask to see my grandson before you die?"

Yes.

"Show me, when I leave off speaking, if you correctly understand what I say. He has been kept unacquainted with the story of his birth. He has no knowledge of it. No suspicion of it. If I bring him here to the side of this bed, he will suppose you to be a perfect stranger. It is more than I can do to keep from him the knowledge that there is such wrong and misery in the world; but that it was ever so near him in his innocent cradle I have kept from him, and I do keep from him, and I ever will keep from him, for his mother's sake, and for his own."

He showed me that he distinctly understood, and the tears fell from his eyes.

"Now rest, and you shall see him."

So I got him a little wine and some brandy, and I put things straight about his bed. But I began to be troubled in my mind lest Jemmy and the Major might be too long of coming back. What with this occupation for my thoughts and hands, I didn't hear a foot upon the stairs, and was startled when I saw the Major stopped short in the middle of the room by the eyes of the man upon the bed, and knowing him then, as I had known him a little while ago.

There was anger in the Major's face, and there was horror and repugnance and I don't know what. So I went up to him and I led him to the bedside, and when I clasped my hands and lifted of them up, the Major did the like.

"O Lord" I says "Thou knowest what we two saw together of the sufferings and sorrows of that young creetur now with Thee. If this dying man is truly penitent, we two together humbly pray Thee to have mercy on him!"

The Major says "Amen!" and then after a little stop I whispers him, "Dear old friend fetch our beloved boy." And the Major, so clever as to have got to understand it all without being told a word, went away and brought him.

Never never never shall I forget the fair bright face of our boy when he stood at the foot of the bed, looking at his unknown father. And O so like his dear young mother then!

"Jemmy" I says, "I have found out all about this poor gentleman who is so ill, and he did lodge in the old house once. And as he wants to see all belonging to it, now that he is passing away, I sent for you."

"Ah poor man!" says Jemmy stepping forward and touching one of his hands with great gentleness. "My heart melts for him. Poor, poor man!"

The eyes that were so soon to close for ever turned to me, and I was not that strong in the pride of my strength that I could resist them.

"My darling boy, there is a reason in the secret history of this fellow-creetur lying as the best and worst of us must all lie one day, which I think would ease his spirit in his last hour if you would lay your cheek against his forehead and say, 'May God forgive you!'"

"O Gran," says Jemmy with a full heart, "I am not worthy!" But he leaned down and did it. Then the faltering fingers made out to catch hold of my sleeve at last, and I believe he was a-trying to kiss me when he died.

* * *

There my dear! There you have the story of my Legacy in full, and it's worth ten times the trouble I have spent upon it if you are pleased to like it.

You might suppose that it set us against the little French town of Sens, but no we didn't find that. I found myself that I never looked up at the high tower atop of the other tower, but the days came back again when that fair young creetur with her pretty bright hair trusted in me like a mother, and the recollection made the place so peaceful to me as I can't express. And every soul about the hotel down to the pigeons in the courtyard made friends with Jemmy and the Major, and went lumbering away with them on all sorts of expeditions in all sorts of vehicles drawn by rampagious cart- horses,--with heads and without,--mud for paint and ropes for harness,--and every new friend dressed in blue like a butcher, and every new horse standing on his hind legs wanting to devour and consume every other horse, and every man that had a whip to crack crack-crack-crack-crack-cracking it as if it was a schoolboy with his first. As to the Major my dear that man lived the greater part of his time with a little tumbler in one hand and a bottle of small wine in the other, and whenever he saw anybody else with a little tumbler, no matter who it was,--the military character with the tags, or the inn-servants at their supper in the courtyard, or townspeople a chatting on a bench, or country people a starting home after market,--down rushes the Major to clink his glass against their glasses and cry,--Hola! Vive Somebody! or Vive Something! as if he was beside himself. And though I could not quite approve of the Major's doing it, still the ways of the world are the ways of the world varying according to the different parts of it, and dancing at all in the open Square with a lady that kept a barber's shop my opinion is that the Major was right to dance his best and to lead off with a power that I did not think was in him, though I was a little uneasy at the Barricading sound of the cries that were set up by the other dancers and the rest of the company, until when I says "What are they ever calling out Jemmy?" Jemmy says, "They're calling out Gran, Bravo the Military English! Bravo the Military English!" which was very gratifying to my feelings as a Briton and became the name the Major was known by.

But every evening at a regular time we all three sat out in the balcony of the hotel at the end of the courtyard, looking up at the golden and rosy light as it changed on the great towers, and looking at the shadows of the towers as they changed on all about us ourselves included, and what do you think we did there? My dear, if Jemmy hadn't brought some other of those stories of the Major's taking down from the telling of former lodgers at Eighty-one Norfolk Street, and if he didn't bring 'em out with this speech:

"Here you are Gran! Here you are godfather! More of 'em! I'll read. And though you wrote 'em for me, godfather, I know you won't disapprove of my making 'em over to Gran; will you?"

"No, my dear boy," says the Major. "Everything we have is hers, and we are hers."

"Hers ever affectionately and devotedly J. Jackman, and J. Jackman Lirriper," cries the Young Rogue giving me a close hug. "Very well then godfather. Look here. As Gran is in the Legacy way just now, I shall make these stories a part of Gran's Legacy. I'll leave 'em to her. What do you say godfather?"

"Hip hip Hurrah!" says the Major.

"Very well then," cries Jemmy all in a bustle. "Vive the Military English! Vive the Lady Lirriper! Vive the Jemmy Jackman Ditto! Vive the Legacy! Now, you look out, Gran. And you look out, godfather. I'LL read! And I'll tell you what I'll do besides. On the last night of our holiday here when we are all packed and going away, I'll top up with something of my own."

"Mind you do sir" says I.

CHAPTER II

--MRS. LIRRIPER RELATES HOW JEMMY TOPPED UP

Well my dear and so the evening readings of those jottings of the Major's brought us round at last to the evening when we were all packed and going away next day, and I do assure you that by that time though it was deliciously comfortable to look forward to the dear old house in Norfolk Street again, I had formed quite a high opinion of the French nation and had noticed them to be much more homely and domestic in their families and far more simple and amiable in their lives than I had ever been led to expect, and it did strike me between ourselves that in one particular they might be imitated to advantage by another nation which I will not mention, and that is in the courage with which they take their little enjoyments on little means and with little things and don't let solemn big-wigs stare them out of countenance or speechify them dull, of which said solemn big-wigs I have ever had the one opinion that I wish they were all made comfortable separately in coppers with the lids on and never let out any more.

"Now young man," I says to Jemmy when we brought our chairs into the balcony that last evening, "you please to remember who was to 'top up.'"

"All right Gran" says Jemmy. "I am the illustrious personage,"

But he looked so serious after he had made me that light answer, that the Major raised his eyebrows at me and I raised mine at the Major.

"Gran and godfather," says Jemmy, "you can hardly think how much my mind has run on Mr. Edson's death."

It gave me a little check. "Ah! it was a sad scene my love" I says, "and sad remembrances come back stronger than merry. But this" I says after a little silence, to rouse myself and the Major and Jemmy all together, "is not topping up. Tell us your story my dear."

"I will" says Jemmy.

"What is the date sir?" says I. "Once upon a time when pigs drank wine?"

"No Gran," says Jemmy, still serious; "once upon a time when the French drank wine."

Again I glanced at the Major, and the Major glanced at me.

"In short, Gran and godfather," says Jemmy, looking up, "the date is this time, and I'm going to tell you Mr. Edson's story."

The flutter that it threw me into. The change of colour on the part of the Major!

"That is to say, you understand," our bright-eyed boy says, "I am going to give you my version of it. I shall not ask whether it's right or not, firstly because you said you knew very little about it, Gran, and secondly because what little you did know was a secret."

I folded my hands in my lap and I never took my eyes off Jemmy as he went running on.

"The unfortunate gentleman" Jemmy commences, "who is the subject of our present narrative was the son of Somebody, and was born Somewhere, and chose a profession Somehow. It is not with those parts of his career that we have to deal; but with his early attachment to a young and beautiful lady."

I thought I should have dropped. I durstn't look at the Major; but I know what his state was, without looking at him.

"The father of our ill-starred hero" says Jemmy, copying as it seemed to me the style of some of his story-books, "was a worldly man who entertained ambitious views for his only son and who firmly set his face against the contemplated alliance with a virtuous but penniless orphan. Indeed he went so far as roundly to assure our hero that unless he weaned his thoughts from the object of his devoted affection, he would disinherit him. At the same time, he proposed as a suitable match the daughter of a neighbouring gentleman of a good estate, who was neither ill-favoured nor unamiable, and whose eligibility in a pecuniary point of view could not be disputed. But young Mr. Edson, true to the first and only love that had inflamed his breast, rejected all considerations of self-advancement, and, deprecating his father's anger in a respectful letter, ran away with her."

My dear I had begun to take a turn for the better, but when it come to running away I began to take another turn for the worse.

"The lovers" says Jemmy "fled to London and were united at the altar of Saint Clement's Danes. And it is at this period of their simple but touching story that we find them inmates of the dwelling of a highly-respected and beloved lady of the name of Gran, residing within a hundred miles of Norfolk Street."

I felt that we were almost safe now, I felt that the dear boy had no suspicion of the bitter truth, and I looked at the Major for the first time and drew a long breath. The Major gave me a nod.

"Our hero's father" Jemmy goes on "proving implacable and carrying his threat into unrelenting execution, the struggles of the young couple in London were severe, and would have been far more so, but for their good angel's having conducted them to the abode of Mrs. Gran; who, divining their poverty (in spite of their endeavours to conceal it from her), by a thousand delicate arts smoothed their rough way, and alleviated the sharpness of their first distress."

Here Jemmy took one of my hands in one of his, and began a marking the turns of his story by making me give a beat from time to time upon his other hand.

"After a while, they left the house of Mrs. Gran, and pursued their fortunes through a variety of successes and failures elsewhere. But in all reverses, whether for good or evil, the words of Mr. Edson to the fair young partner of his life were, 'Unchanging Love and Truth will carry us through all!'"

My hand trembled in the dear boy's, those words were so wofully unlike the fact.

"Unchanging Love and Truth" says Jemmy over again, as if he had a proud kind of a noble pleasure in it, "will carry us through all! Those were his words. And so they fought their way, poor but gallant and happy, until Mrs. Edson gave birth to a child."

"A daughter," I says.

"No," says Jemmy, "a son. And the father was so proud of it that he could hardly bear it out of his sight. But a dark cloud overspread the scene. Mrs. Edson sickened, drooped, and died."

"Ah! Sickened, drooped, and died!" I says.

"And so Mr. Edson's only comfort, only hope on earth, and only stimulus to action, was his darling boy. As the child grew older, he grew so like his mother that he was her living picture. It used to make him wonder why his father cried when he kissed him. But unhappily he was like his mother in constitution as well as in face, and lo, died too before he had grown out of childhood. Then Mr. Edson, who had good abilities, in his forlornness and despair, threw them all to the winds. He became apathetic, reckless, lost. Little by little he sank down, down, down, down, until at last he almost lived (I think) by gaming. And so sickness overtook him in the town of Sens in France, and he lay down to die. But now that he laid him down when all was done, and looked back upon the green Past beyond the time when he had covered it with ashes, he thought gratefully of the good Mrs. Gran long lost sight of, who had been so kind to him and his young wife in the early days of their marriage, and he left the little that he had as a last Legacy to her. And she, being brought to see him, at first no more knew him than she would know from seeing the ruin of a Greek or Roman Temple, what it used to be before it fell; but at length she remembered him. And then he told her, with tears, of his regret for the misspent part of his life, and besought her to think as mildly of it as she could, because it was the poor fallen Angel of his unchanging Love and Constancy after all. And because she had her grandson with her, and he fancied that his own boy, if he had lived, might have grown to be something like him, he asked her to let him touch his forehead with his cheek and say certain parting words."

Jemmy's voice sank low when it got to that, and tears filled my eyes, and filled the Major's.

"You little Conjurer" I says, "how did you ever make it all out? Go in and write it every word down, for it's a wonder."

Which Jemmy did, and I have repeated it to you my dear from his writing.

Then the Major took my hand and kissed it, and said, "Dearest madam all has prospered with us."

"Ah Major" I says drying my eyes, "we needn't have been afraid. We might have known it. Treachery don't come natural to beaming youth; but trust and pity, love and constancy,--they do, thank God!"

Charles Dickens

Charles John Huffam Dickens (/ˈtʃɑrlz ˈdɪkɪnz/; 7 February 1812 – 9 June 1870) was an English writer and social critic. He created some of the world's best-known fictional characters and is regarded as the greatest novelist of the Victorian era.[1] His works enjoyed unprecedented popularity during his lifetime, and by the twentieth century critics and scholars had recognised him as a literary genius. His novels and short stories enjoy lasting popularity.[2][3]

Born in Portsmouth, Dickens left school to work in a factory when his father was incarcerated in a debtors' prison. Despite his lack of formal education, he edited a weekly journal for 20 years, wrote 15 novels, five novellas, hundreds of short stories and non-fiction articles, lectured and performed extensively, was an indefatigable letter writer, and campaigned vigorously for children's rights, education, and other social reforms.

Dickens's literary success began with the 1836 serial publication of The Pickwick Papers. Within a few years he had become an international literary celebrity, famous for his humour, satire, and keen observation of character and society. His novels, most published in monthly or weekly instalments, pioneered the serial publication of narrative fiction, which became the dominant Victorian mode for novel publication.[4][5] The instalment format allowed Dickens to evaluate his audience's reaction, and he often modified his plot and character development based on such feedback.[5] For example, when his wife's chiropodist expressed distress at the way Miss Mowcher in David Copperfield seemed to reflect her disabilities, Dickens improved the character with positive features.[6] His plots were carefully constructed, and he often wove elements from topical events into his narratives.[7] Masses of the illiterate poor chipped in ha'pennies to have each new monthly episode read to them, opening up and inspiring a new class of readers.[8]

Dickens was regarded as the literary colossus of his age.[9] His 1843 novella, A Christmas Carol, remains popular and continues to inspire adaptations in every artistic genre. Oliver Twist and Great Expectations are also frequently adapted, and, like many of his novels, evoke images of early Victorian London. His 1859 novel, A Tale of Two Cities, set in London and Paris, is his best-known work of historical fiction. Dickens's creative genius has been praised by fellow writers—from Leo Tolstoy to George Orwell and G. K. Chesterton—for its realism, comedy, prose style, unique characterisations, and social criticism. On the other hand, Oscar Wilde, Henry James, and Virginia Woolf complained of a lack of psychological depth, loose writing, and a vein of saccharine sentimentalism. The term Dickensian is used to describe something that is reminiscent of Dickens and his writings, such as poor social conditions or comically repulsive characters.[10]

Early years

Charles John Huffam Dickens was born on 7 February 1812, at 1 Mile End Terrace (now 393 Commercial Road), Landport in Portsea Island (Portsmouth), the second of eight children of John Dickens (1785–1851) and Elizabeth Dickens (née Barrow; 1789–1863). His father was a clerk in the Navy Pay Office and was temporarily stationed in the district. He asked Christopher Huffam,[12] rigger to His Majesty's Navy, gentleman, and head of an established firm, to act as godfather to Charles. Huffam is thought to be the inspiration for Paul Dombey, the owner of a shipping company in Dickens's eponymous Dombey and Son (1848).[12]

In January 1815 John Dickens was called back to London, and the family moved to Norfolk Street, Fitzrovia.[13] When Charles was four, they relocated to Sheerness, and thence to Chatham, Kent, where he spent his formative years until the age of 11. His early life seems to have been idyllic, though he thought himself a "very small and not-over-particularly-taken-care-of boy".[14]

Charles spent time outdoors but also read voraciously, including the picaresque novels of Tobias Smollett and Henry Fielding, as well as Robinson Crusoe and Gil Blas. He read and reread The Arabian Nights and the Collected Farces of Elizabeth Inchbald.[15] He retained poignant memories of childhood, helped by an excellent memory of people and events, which he used in his writing.[16] His father's brief work as a clerk in the Navy Pay Office afforded him a few years of private education, first at a dame school, and then at a school run by William Giles, a dissenter, in Chatham.[17]

This period came to an end in June 1822, when John Dickens was recalled to Navy Pay Office headquarters at Somerset House, and the family—minus Charles, who stayed behind to finish his final term of work—moved to Camden Town in London.[19] The family had left Kent amidst rapidly mounting debts, and, living beyond his means,[20] John Dickens was forced by his creditors into the Marshalsea debtors' prison in Southwark, London in 1824. His wife and youngest children joined him there, as was the practice at the time. Charles, then 12 years old, boarded with Elizabeth Roylance, a family friend, at 112 College Place, Camden Town.[21] Roylance was "a reduced [impoverished] old lady, long known to our family", whom Dickens later immortalised, "with a few alterations and embellishments", as "Mrs. Pipchin" in Dombey and Son. Later, he lived in a back-attic in the house of an agent for the Insolvent Court, Archibald Russell, "a fat, good-natured, kind old gentleman... with a quiet old wife" and lame son, in Lant Street in Southwark.[22] They provided the inspiration for the Garlands in The Old Curiosity Shop.[23]

On Sundays—with his sister Frances, free from her studies at the Royal Academy of Music—he spent the day at the Marshalsea.[24] Dickens later used the prison as a setting in Little Dorrit. To pay for his board and to help his family, Dickens was forced to leave school and work ten-hour days at Warren's Blacking Warehouse, on Hungerford Stairs, near the present

Charing Cross railway station, where he earned six shillings a week pasting labels on pots of boot blacking. The strenuous and often harsh working conditions made a lasting impression on Dickens and later influenced his fiction and essays, becoming the foundation of his interest in the reform of socio-economic and labour conditions, the rigours of which he believed were unfairly borne by the poor. He later wrote that he wondered "how I could have been so easily cast away at such an age".[25] As he recalled to John Forster (from The Life of Charles Dickens):

The blacking-warehouse was the last house on the left-hand side of the way, at old Hungerford Stairs. It was a crazy, tumble-down old house, abutting of course on the river, and literally overrun with rats. Its wainscoted rooms, and its rotten floors and staircase, and the old grey rats swarming down in the cellars, and the sound of their squeaking and scuffling coming up the stairs at all times, and the dirt and decay of the place, rise up visibly before me, as if I were there again. The counting-house was on the first floor, looking over the coal-barges and the river. There was a recess in it, in which I was to sit and work. My work was to cover the pots of paste-blacking; first with a piece of oil-paper, and then with a piece of blue paper; to tie them round with a string; and then to clip the paper close and neat, all round, until it looked as smart as a pot of ointment from an apothecary's shop. When a certain number of grosses of pots had attained this pitch of perfection, I was to paste on each a printed label, and then go on again with more pots. Two or three other boys were kept at similar duty down-stairs on similar wages. One of them came up, in a ragged apron and a paper cap, on the first Monday morning, to show me the trick of using the string and tying the knot. His name was Bob Fagin; and I took the liberty of using his name, long afterwards, in Oliver Twist.[25]

When the warehouse was moved to Chandos Street in the smart, busy district of Covent Garden the boys worked in a room in which the window gave onto the street and little audiences gathered and watched them at work—in Dickens biographer Simon Callow's estimation, the public display was "a new refinement added to his misery".[26]

The Marshalsea around 1897, after it had closed

A few months after his imprisonment, John Dickens' paternal grandmother, Elizabeth Dickens, died and bequeathed him £450. On the expectation of this legacy, Dickens was released from prison. Under the Insolvent Debtors Act, Dickens arranged for payment of his creditors, and he and his family left Marshalsea,[27] for the home of Mrs Roylance.

Charles's mother, Elizabeth Dickens, did not immediately support his removal from the boot-blacking warehouse. This influenced Dickens' view that a father should rule the family, and a mother find her proper sphere inside the home: "I never afterwards forgot, I never shall forget, I never can forget, that my mother was warm for my being sent back". His mother's failure to request his return was a factor in his dissatisfied attitude towards women.[28]

Righteous indignation stemming from his own situation and the conditions under which working-class people lived became major themes of his works, and it was this unhappy period in his youth to which he alluded in his favourite, and most autobiographical, novel, David Copperfield:[29] "I had no advice, no counsel, no encouragement, no consolation, no assistance, no support, of any kind, from anyone, that I can call to mind, as I hope to go to heaven!"[30]

Dickens was eventually sent to the Wellington House Academy in Camden Town, where he remained until March 1827, having spent about two years there. He did not consider it to be a good school: "Much of the haphazard, desultory teaching, poor discipline punctuated by the headmaster's sadistic brutality, the seedy ushers and general run-down atmosphere, are embodied in Mr. Creakle's Establishment in David Copperfield."[30]

Dickens worked at the law office of Ellis and Blackmore, attorneys, of Holborn Court, Gray's Inn, as a junior clerk from May 1827 to November 1828. He was a gifted mimic and impersonated those around him: clients, lawyers, and clerks. He went to theatres obsessively—he claimed that for at least three years he went to the theatre every single day. His favourite actor was Charles

Mathews, and Dickens learnt his monopolylogues, (farces in which Mathews played every character), by heart.[31] Then, having learned Gurney's system of shorthand in his spare time, he left to become a freelance reporter. A distant relative, Thomas Charlton, was a freelance reporter at Doctors' Commons, and Dickens was able to share his box there to report the legal proceedings for nearly four years.[32][33] This education was to inform works such as Nicholas Nickleby, Dombey and Son, and especially Bleak House— whose vivid portrayal of the machinations and bureaucracy of the legal system did much to enlighten the general public and served as a vehicle for dissemination of Dickens's own views regarding, particularly, the heavy burden on the poor who were forced by circumstances to "go to law".

In 1830, Dickens met his first love, Maria Beadnell, thought to have been the model for the character Dora in David Copperfield. Maria's parents disapproved of the courtship and ended the relationship by sending her to school in Paris.[34]

Journalism and early novels

In 1832, at age 20, Dickens was energetic and increasingly self-confident.[35] He enjoyed mimicry and popular entertainment, lacked a clear, specific sense of what he wanted to become, and yet knew he wanted fame. Drawn to the theatre—he became an early member of the Garrick[36]—he landed an acting audition at Covent Garden, where the manager George Bartley and the actor Charles Kemble were to see him. Dickens prepared meticulously and decided to imitate the comedian Charles Mathews, but ultimately he missed the audition because of a cold. Before another opportunity arose, he had set out on his career as a writer.[37] In 1833 he submitted his first story, "A Dinner at Poplar Walk", to the London periodical Monthly Magazine.[38] William Barrow, a brother of his mother, offered him a job on The Mirror of Parliament and he worked in the House of Commons for the first time early in 1832. He rented rooms at Furnival's Inn and worked as a political journalist, reporting on Parliamentary debates, and he travelled across Britain to cover election campaigns for the Morning Chronicle. His journalism, in the form of sketches in periodicals, formed his first collection of pieces, published in 1836: Sketches by Boz—Boz being a family nickname he employed as a pseudonym for some years.[39][40] Dickens apparently adopted it from the nickname "Moses", which he had given to his youngest brother Augustus Dickens, after a character in Oliver Goldsmith's The Vicar of Wakefield. When pronounced by anyone with a head cold, "Moses" became "Boses"—later shortened to Boz.[40][41] Dickens's own name was considered "queer" by a contemporary critic, who wrote in 1849: "Mr Dickens, as if in revenge for his own queer name, does bestow still queerer ones upon his fictitious creations." He contributed to and edited journals throughout his literary career.[38] In January 1835 the Morning Chronicle launched an evening edition, under the editorship of the Chronicle's music critic, George Hogarth. Hogarth invited Dickens to contribute Street Sketches and Dickens became a regular visitor to his Fulham house, excited by Hogarth's friendship with a hero of his, Walter Scott, and enjoying the company of Hogarth's three daughters—Georgina, Mary, and nineteen-year-old Catherine.[42]

Catherine Hogarth Dickens by Samuel Lawrence (1838)
Dickens made rapid progress both professionally and socially. He began a friendship with William Harrison Ainsworth, the author of the highwayman novel Rookwood (1834), whose bachelor salon in Harrow Road had become the meeting place for a set that included Daniel Maclise, Benjamin Disraeli, Edward Bulwer-Lytton, and George Cruikshank. All these became his friends and collaborators, with the exception of Disraeli, and he met his first publisher, John Macrone, at the house.[43] The success of Sketches by Boz led to a proposal from publishers Chapman and Hall for Dickens to supply text to match Robert Seymour's engraved illustrations in a monthly letterpress. Seymour committed suicide after the second instalment, and Dickens, who wanted to write a connected series of sketches, hired "Phiz" to provide the engravings (which were reduced from four to two per instalment) for the story. The resulting story became The Pickwick Papers, and though the first few episodes were not successful, the introduction of the Cockney character Sam Weller in the fourth episode (the first to be illustrated by Phiz) marked a sharp climb in its popularity.[44] The final instalment sold 40,000 copies.[38]

In November 1836 Dickens accepted the position of editor of Bentley's Miscellany, a position he held for three years, until he fell out with the owner.[45] In 1836 as he finished the last instalments of The Pickwick Papers, he began writing the beginning instalments of Oliver Twist—writing as many as 90 pages a month—while continuing work on Bentley's and also writing four plays, the production of which he oversaw. Oliver Twist, published in 1838, became one of Dickens's better known stories, and was the first Victorian novel with a child protagonist.[46]

Young Charles Dickens by Daniel Maclise (1839)
On 2 April 1836, after a one-year engagement, and between episodes two and three of The Pickwick Papers, Dickens married Catherine Thomson Hogarth (1816–1879), the daughter of George Hogarth, editor of the Evening Chronicle.[47] After a brief honeymoon in Chalk in Kent the couple returned to lodgings at Furnival's Inn.[48] The first of their ten children, Charley, was born in January 1837, and a few months later the family set up home in Bloomsbury at 48 Doughty Street, London, (on which Charles had a three-year lease at £80 a year) from 25 March 1837 until December 1839.[47][49] Dickens's younger brother Frederick and Catherine's 17-year-old sister Mary, moved in with them. Dickens became very attached to Mary, and she died in his arms after a brief illness in 1837. Unusually for Dickens, as a consequence of his shock, he stopped working, and he and Kate stayed at a little farm on Hampstead Heath for a fortnight. Dickens idealised Mary,- the character he fashioned after her, Rose Maylie, he found he could not now kill, as he had planned, in his fiction[50] and according to Ackroyd he drew on memories of her for his later descriptions of Little Nell and Florence Dombey.[51] His grief was so great that he was unable to meet the deadline for the June instalment of Pickwick Papers and had to cancel the Oliver Twist instalment that month as well.[46] The time in Hampstead was the occasion for a growing bond between Dickens and John Forster to develop and Forster soon became his unofficial business manager, and the first to read his work.[52]

Barnaby Rudge was Dickens's first popular failure—but the character of Dolly

Varden, "pretty, witty, sexy, became central to numerous theatrical adaptations"[53]

His success as a novelist continued. The young Queen Victoria read both Oliver Twist and Pickwick, staying up until midnight to discuss them.[54] Nicholas Nickleby (1838–39), The Old Curiosity Shop and, finally, his first historical novel, Barnaby Rudge: A Tale of the Riots of 'Eighty, as part of the Master Humphrey's Clock series (1840–41), were all published in monthly instalments before being made into books.[55]

In the midst of all his activity during this period there was discontent with his publishers and John Macrone was bought off, while Richard Bentley signed over all his rights in Oliver Twist. Other illustrations of a certain restlessness and discontent emerge—in Broadstairs he flirted with Eleanor Picken, the young fiancée of his solicitor's best friend, and one night grabbed her and ran with her down to the sea. He declared they were both to drown there in the "sad sea waves". She finally got free but afterwards kept her distance. In June 1841 he precipitately set out on a two-month tour of Scotland and then, in September 1841, telegraphed Forster that he had decided to go to America.[56] Master Humphrey's Clock was shut down, though Dickens was still keen on the idea of the weekly magazine, a form he liked, a liking that had begun with his childhood reading of the eighteenth-century magazines Tatler and The Spectator.

First visit to the United States

In 1842, Dickens and his wife made their first trip to the United States and Canada. At this time Georgina Hogarth, another sister of Catherine, joined the Dickens household, now living at Devonshire Terrace, Marylebone, to care for the young family they had left behind.[57] She remained with them as housekeeper, organiser, adviser, and friend until Dickens's death in 1870.[58]

Sketch of Dickens in 1842 during American Tour. Sketch of Dickens's sister Fanny, bottom left

He described his impressions in a travelogue, American Notes for General

Circulation. Dickens includes in Notes a powerful condemnation of slavery, which he had attacked as early as The Pickwick Papers, correlating the emancipation of the poor in England with the abolition of slavery abroad[59] citing newspaper accounts of runaway slaves disfigured by their masters. From Richmond, Virginia Dickens returned to Washington, D.C. and started a trek westward to St. Louis. While there, he expressed a desire to see an American prairie before returning east. A group of 13 men then set out with Dickens to visit Looking Glass Prairie, a trip 30 miles into Illinois.

During his visit, Dickens spent a month in New York City, giving lectures, raising the question of international copyright laws and the pirating of his work in America.[60][61] He persuaded a group of twenty-five writers, headed by Washington Irving, to sign a petition for him to take to Congress, but the press were generally hostile to this, saying that he should be grateful for his popularity and that it was mercenary to complain about his work being pirated.[62]

The popularity he gained caused a shift in his self-perception according to critic Kate Flint, who writes the he "found himself a cultural commodity, and its circulation had passed out his control", causing him to become interested in and delve into themes of public and personal personas in the next novels.[63] She writes that he assumed a role of "influential commentator", publicly and in his fiction, evident in his next few books.[63]

Soon after his return to England, Dickens began work on the first of his Christmas stories, A Christmas Carol, written in 1843, which was followed by The Chimes in 1844 and The Cricket on the Hearth in 1845. Of these, A Christmas Carol was most popular and, tapping into an old tradition, did much to promote a renewed enthusiasm for the joys of Christmas in Britain and America.[64] The seeds for the story became planted in Dickens's mind during a trip to Manchester to witness the conditions of the manufacturing workers there. This, along with scenes he had recently witnessed at the Field Lane Ragged School, caused Dickens to resolve to "strike a sledge hammer blow" for the poor. As the idea for the story took shape and the writing began in earnest, Dickens became engrossed in the book. He later wrote that as the tale unfolded he "wept and laughed, and wept again" as he "walked about the black streets of London fifteen or twenty miles many a night when all sober folks had gone to bed."[65]

After living briefly in Italy (1844), Dickens travelled to Switzerland (1846), where he began work on Dombey and Son (1846–48). This and David Copperfield (1849–50) mark a significant artistic break in Dickens's career as his novels became more serious in theme and more carefully planned than his early works.

Philanthropy

In May 1846 Angela Burdett Coutts, heir to the Coutts banking fortune, approached Dickens about setting up a home for the redemption of fallen women of the working class. Coutts envisioned a home that would replace the punitive regimes of existing institutions with a reformative environment conducive to education and proficiency in domestic household chores. After initially resisting, Dickens eventually founded the home, named "Urania Cottage", in the Lime Grove section of Shepherds Bush, which he managed for ten years,[66] setting the house rules, reviewing the accounts and interviewing prospective residents.[67] Emigration and marriage were central to Dickens's agenda for the women on leaving Urania Cottage, from which it is estimated that about 100 women graduated between 1847 and 1859.[68]

Religious views

As a young man Dickens expressed a distaste for certain aspects of organized religion. In 1836, in a pamphlet titled Sunday Under Three Heads, he defended the people's right to pleasure, opposing a plan to prohibit games on Sundays. "Look into your churches- diminished congregations and scanty attendance. People have grown sullen and obstinate, and are becoming disgusted with the faith which condemns them to such a day as this, once in every seven. They display their feeling by staying away [from church]. Turn into the streets [on a Sunday] and mark the rigid gloom that reigns over everything around"[69]

Dickens honoured the figure of Christ —though he denied his divinity.[70] Notwithstanding, Dickens has been characterized as a professing Christian.[71] His son Henry Fielding Dickens described Dickens as someone who "possessed deep religious convictions". Though in the early 1840s Dickens had showed an interest in Unitarian Christianity, the writer Gary Colledge has asserted that he 'never strayed from his attachment to popular lay Anglicanism.'[72] He also wrote a religious work called The Life of Our Lord (1849), which was a short book about the life of Jesus Christ, written with the purpose of inculcating his faith to his children and family.[73][74]

Dickens disapproved of Roman Catholicism and 19th-century evangelicalism, and was critical of what he saw as the hypocrisy of religious institutions and philosophies like spiritualism, all of which he considered deviations from the true spirit of Christianity.[75] Leo Tolstoy and Fyodor Dostoyevsky referred to Dickens as "that great Christian writer".[76][77]

Middle years

"Little Dorrit" 1856
In late November 1851, Dickens moved into Tavistock House where he wrote Bleak House (1852–53), Hard Times (1854) and Little Dorrit (1856).[78] It was here that he indulged in the amateur theatricals described in Forster's "Life".[79] During this period he worked closely with the novelist and playwright Wilkie Collins. In 1856, his income from writing allowed him to buy Gad's Hill Place in Higham, Kent. As a child, Dickens had walked past the house and dreamed of living in it. The area was also the scene of some of the events of Shakespeare's Henry IV, Part 1, and this literary connection pleased him.[80]

Ellen Ternan, 1858
In 1857, Dickens hired professional actresses for the play The Frozen Deep,

written by him and his protégé, Wilkie Collins. Dickens fell deeply in love with one of the actresses, Ellen Ternan, and this passion was to last the rest of his life.[81] Dickens was 45 and Ternan 18 when he made the decision, which went strongly against Victorian convention, to separate from his wife, Catherine, in 1858—divorce was still unthinkable for someone as famous as he was. When Catherine left, never to see her husband again, she took with her one child, leaving the other children to be raised by her sister Georgina who chose to stay at Gad's Hill.[58]

During this period, whilst pondering a project to give public readings for his own profit, Dickens was approached through a charitable appeal by Great Ormond Street Hospital, to help it survive its first major financial crisis. His 'Drooping Buds' essay in Household Words earlier in 3 April 1852 was considered by the hospital's founders to have been the catalyst for the hospital's success.[82] Dickens, whose philanthropy was well-known, was asked by his friend, the hospital's founder Charles West, to preside over the appeal, and he threw himself into the task, heart and soul.[83] Dickens's public readings secured sufficient funds for an endowment to put the hospital on a sound financial footing—one reading on 9 February 1858 alone raised £3,000.[84][85][86]

After separating from Catherine,[87] Dickens undertook a series of hugely popular and remunerative reading tours which, together with his journalism, were to absorb most of his creative energies for the next decade, in which he was to write only two more novels.[88] His first reading tour, lasting from April 1858 to February 1859, consisted of 129 appearances in 49 different towns throughout England, Scotland and Ireland.[89] Dickens's continued fascination with the theatrical world was written into the theatre scenes in Nicholas Nickleby, but more importantly he found an outlet in public readings. In 1866, he undertook a series of public readings in England and Scotland, with more the following year in England and Ireland.

At his desk in 1858
Major works soon followed, including A Tale of Two Cities (1859) and Great

Expectations (1861), which were resounding successes. During this time he was also the publisher, editor, and a major contributor to the journals Household Words (1850–1859) and All the Year Round (1858–1870).[90]

In early September 1860, in a field behind Gad's Hill, Dickens made a bonfire of most of his correspondence—only those letters on business matters were spared. Since Ellen Ternan also destroyed all of his letters to her,[91] the extent of the affair between the two remains speculative.[92] In the 1930s, Thomas Wright recounted that Ternan had unburdened herself with a Canon Benham, and gave currency to rumours they had been lovers.[93] That the two had a son who died in infancy was alleged by Dickens's daughter, Kate Perugini, whom Gladys Storey had interviewed before her death in 1929. Storey published her account in Dickens and Daughter,[94][95] but no contemporary evidence exists. On his death, Dickens settled an annuity on Ternan which made her a financially independent woman. Claire Tomalin's book, The Invisible Woman, argues that Ternan lived with Dickens secretly for the last 13 years of his life. The book was subsequently turned into a play, Little Nell, by Simon Gray, and a 2013 film.

In the same period, Dickens furthered his interest in the paranormal, becoming one of the early members of The Ghost Club.[96]

In June 1862 he was offered £10,000 for a reading tour of Australia.[97] He was enthusiastic, and even planned a travel book, The Uncommercial Traveller Upside Down, but ultimately decided against the tour.[98] Two of his sons— Alfred D'Orsay Tennyson Dickens and Edward Bulwer Lytton Dickens—migrated to Australia, Edward becoming a member of the Parliament of New South Wales as Member for Wilcannia 1889–94.[99][100]

Last years

After the Staplehurst rail crash
On 9 June 1865, while returning from Paris with Ellen Ternan, Dickens was involved in the Staplehurst rail crash. The train's first seven carriages plunged

off a cast iron bridge that was under repair, The only first-class carriage to remain on the track was the one in which Dickens was travelling. Before rescuers arrived, Dickens tended and comforted the wounded and the dying with a flask of brandy and a hat refreshed with water, and saved some lives. Before leaving, he remembered the unfinished manuscript for Our Mutual Friend, and he returned to his carriage to retrieve it.[101] Dickens later used this experience as material for his short ghost story, "The Signal-Man", in which the central character has a premonition of his own death in a rail crash. He also based the story on several previous rail accidents, such as the Clayton Tunnel rail crash of 1861. Dickens managed to avoid an appearance at the inquest to avoid disclosing that he had been travelling with Ternan and her mother, which would have caused a scandal.[102]

Second visit to the United States

In the late 1850s Dickens began to contemplate a second visit to the United States, tempted by the money that he believed he could make by extending his reading tour there. The outbreak of the Civil War in America in 1861 delayed his plans. Over two years after the war, Dickens set sail from Liverpool on 9 November 1867 for his second American reading tour. Landing at Boston, he devoted the rest of the month to a round of dinners with such notables as Ralph Waldo Emerson, Henry Wadsworth Longfellow and his American publisher James Thomas Fields. In early December, the readings began. He performed 76 readings, netting £19,000, from December 1867 to April 1868.[103] Dickens shuttled between Boston and New York, where he gave 22 readings at Steinway Hall. Although he had started to suffer from what he called the "true American catarrh", he kept to a schedule that would have challenged a much younger man, even managing to squeeze in some sleighing in Central Park.

Poster promoting a reading by Dickens in Nottingham dated 4 February 1869, two months before he suffered a mild stroke

During his travels, he saw a significant change in the people and the circumstances of America. His final appearance was at a banquet the

American Press held in his honour at Delmonico's on 18 April, when he promised never to denounce America again. By the end of the tour, the author could hardly manage solid food, subsisting on champagne and eggs beaten in sherry. On 23 April, he boarded his ship to return to Britain, barely escaping a Federal Tax Lien against the proceeds of his lecture tour.[104]

Farewell readings

Between 1868 and 1869, Dickens gave a series of "farewell readings" in England, Scotland, and Ireland, beginning on 6 October. He managed, of a contracted 100 readings, to deliver 75 in the provinces, with a further 12 in London.[103] As he pressed on he was affected by giddiness and fits of paralysis and collapsed on 22 April 1869, at Preston in Lancashire, and on doctor's advice, the tour was cancelled.[105] After further provincial readings were cancelled, he began work on his final novel, The Mystery of Edwin Drood. It was fashionable in the 1860s to 'do the slums' and, in company, Dickens visited opium dens in Shadwell, where he witnessed an elderly addict known as "Laskar Sal", who formed the model for the "Opium Sal" subsequently featured in his mystery novel, Edwin Drood.[106]

After Dickens had regained sufficient strength, he arranged, with medical approval, for a final series of readings to partially make up to his sponsors what they had lost due to his illness. There were to be 12 performances, running between 11 January and 15 March 1870, the last at 8:00 pm at St. James's Hall in London. Although in grave health by this time, he read A Christmas Carol and The Trial from Pickwick. On 2 May, he made his last public appearance at a Royal Academy Banquet in the presence of the Prince and Princess of Wales, paying a special tribute on the death of his friend, the illustrator Daniel Maclise.[107]

Death

Samuel Luke Fildes—The Empty Chair. Fildes was illustrating "Edwin Drood" at the time of Charles Dickens's death. The engraving shows Dickens's empty chair in his study at Gads Hill Place. It appeared in the Christmas 1870 edition of the The Graphic and thousands of prints of it were sold.[108]

Printed in Poland
by Amazon Fulfillment
Poland Sp. z o.o., Wrocław